Rose City Ink

Presents...

No Loyalty No Love

2

Written By,

Shelli Marie

&

Summer Grant

Printed in the USA

Publisher: Rose City Ink

Editor: Shelli Marie

No Loyalty, No Love 2

ACKNOWLEDGEMENTS

(SHELLI MARIE)

To God Almighty I give the glory.

To my Sis Summer Grant, thanks a million for doing this project with me!

To my family support team:
Jeremy, Jessica, Danielle, Vassie Jr., Jaden, Tianna, Journey and Thalia.
Thanks for all of your encouragement.
I love you guys! Always!!

To the rest of the Dishman Klan: Jennifer Dishman, Kim Dishman, Marlo and Devin Dishman
Daddy and Genora Dishman
I love you all dearly!!

To my extended support team: My Sis JeaNida Luckie-Weatherall, My Sissy Teruka B, My Boo JC (J Criss), BFF Sheila James, BFF TonYelle Reese- Britt, My Niecey Alexys "Chelle" Price, My Sis Robin Temple, My Sis Denise Henson, My Cuddy Craig Price... Thanks!

SPECIAL THANKS TO ALL MY ROSE CITY READERS!!
MUCH LOVE... ALWAYS
JeaNida Luckie-Weatherall, MzNicki Ervin, Miko
Covington, Tiarra Neely, Alisha Simko, Toya Merrit,
Kim Turner, Rebecca Rodgers, Scarlett Brock,
Chanell McPherson, Kierre Moore, Stephania Hurst,
Anita Wiley and Andrea Provost.
Toni Futrell, Real Queen B Divas, Koko Kreme, Mita
Rhodes, Delores Miles, Latasha 'Shine' Mack, My
Sis Denise Henson, LaToya Crump, Junanya Shiel,
Nikki Williams, Rahmah Chaplin, Mellissia
DeShields, Authoress Divine Six, Cheryl Hayes,
GoddessLove Author MsMeka, Janelia Brooks,
MizzLadii Redd, Nyaisia, Hadiyah Salim, Karen Day-
Wright, Phyllis Keith-Young, Patricia Charles, Allisha
Bethel, Camille Joy Mackey, Shay Chisadza, Bwn
Eyz, Tanisha Reed, Chanell Johnson, Tonya
Robinson, Lynette Anderson, Cyndy Twin, Jamie
Holmes, Stephanie Wiley, Karen Wiley, Ambria
Davis, Candy Rain, Sandra Payton Nettles, Carolyn
McCauley, Ramon Lowe, Sean Scott, Sonia
Williams, Tamisha Dixon, Nancy Santana Gambino,
Nikey Craig, Ebony Sims, Malika Jones, Nicki Ervin,
Luciana Monroe, Quaran Owens, Charlotte Martin,
Charles Fulton, Debra Campbell Curry, Stacy Phifer

Mills, and all the rest of you! If I didn't mention your name, blame it on my head and not my heart!

ACKNOWLEDGEMENTS

(SUMMER GRANT)

I hope that you all enjoy this series. Thank you guys so much for supporting us. I appreciate it from the bottom of my heart. Summer Grant

DEDICATION

This book is dedicated to all the struggling authors out there stepping out on faith...

Don't Give Up, God Gotcha!

Recap

Book 1

Trent walked off up to his room to take a call. I was exhausted from all the bullshit I had been going through over the past few weeks. I stayed downstairs and went into the family room to cut on the television. I needed a distraction and watching some Law & Order, Criminal Minds, or Shades of Blue was just the thing to do it.

I drew the blinds closed to make it nice and dark. I then grabbed a blanket off of the nearby chair and went to get cozy on the nice comfortable sectional. It was softer than anything that I had ever laid on.

After snuggling into the pillow, I flicked through the channels.

"Dy, Dylasia," Trent yelled out.

"What does he want now?" I huffed. Shit I was just getting comfortable and I didn't want to get up.

"What?" I hollered back hoping that he would come to me."

When he didn't, I went ahead and stood up to head towards the staircase. "What Trent?"

"Ding, dong"

The doorbell rang a couple of times and at the same time Trent came running down the stairs taking two at a time.

"Don't answer that!" he shouted with a terrified expression.

He had his gun drawn and had it pointed at the front door where I was standing.

"What's going on?" I shouted as I ran towards him.

All in one motion, Trent placed his body in front of mine and took the two bullets that shot right through the door. "Ugh"

Trent began gasping for air as he hit the stairs. I took the cold steel from him and began firing away until there was no more ammo in the gun.

I dropped the weapon and bent down to check on Trent. That was when I felt a burning pain in my side. Hesitantly I looked down only to see that I was shot as well.

"Dy, go get my phone…" Trent whispered as he held on to his chest.

"Okay," I grunted through the pain as I heard a crashing noise behind me.

"Watch out!" he warned as he held on to my arms so tightly that he was about to cut off my circulation.

"What's wrong?" I questioned trying to pry his hands away.

Trent's terrified focus went from me to something or someone behind me. I couldn't even turn around to see before I felt someone grab me by my ankles and pull me forcefully.

"Don't let me go!" I cried to Trent as his grip began to loosen.

First it was my right hand. "No!"

I quickly used it to get a hold of the railing below the banister. "Don't let me go Trent!"

Trent's eyes widened as they started to water. Seconds later his grip on my left wrist slipped.

"No!" I screamed as my body was drug from Trent's house against my will.

The whole front of my body felt like it was being skinned. The tiny pieces of gravel from the ground were being embedded into my legs, chest, stomach and palms.

"Stop, get your fucking hands off of me! Let me go!" I hollered as the person flipped me over onto my back. "What the hell?"

I couldn't believe who it was. I didn't understand.

"Why the hell are you doing this?" I cried. "What the fuck did I ever do to you?"

Instead of an answer, I received a mighty blow. That motherfucker was hard enough to knock me completely the fuck out.

Chapter 1

"Aaarrgh!" I winced in pain while being jerked awake. My insides were feeling like they were on fire.

I couldn't see anything, and my jaw was banging like I got slapped with a ton of bricks. The pain was so intense that I was on the verge of passing out again.

As I attempted to shift my body, the stench of old feces and live flesh invaded my nostrils. The smell was so vile, I instantly became nauseous.

Adjusting my eyes to the darkness, I continued to try to move my hands and legs.

Nothing happened and that was when the panic started to set in.

Suddenly, flashes of Trent being shot crossed my mind. I instantly became real nervous.

"Trent!" I shouted causing my voice to echo.

"Where the fuck am I?" I wondered out loud. I couldn't see shit. The cold damp concrete floor led me to believe that I was in a basement or an abandoned building. Wherever it was, I needed to find out because I had to get me some damn help.

Trying my best to lean forward, a sharp pain shot up the side of my rib. I didn't know what was causing it and the darkness made it impossible to find out at the moment.

"Owww…. Help me please!" I pleaded as my body suddenly felt numb.

A bright fluorescent light came on and I immediately searched my surroundings. "I knew it!"

I was in some type of utility basement. Old blinds, dry wall, plastic rolls, paint and tools were scattered throughout the room.

Looking down, I noticed my shirt was soaked in blood. That was what was making me so damn cold.

"Who the hell is that?" I panicked as I heard footsteps and voices approaching.

"What the fuck did y'all do to her?!" Rick shouted to Ivery and Sydney. "I told y'all that I would stay quiet about this shit but kidnapping folks is taking this shit way too far! Look, she's about to bleed to fucking death!"

"Awwwww, that bitch is alright!" Ivery smirked. "She is about to learn a lesson today and I'm gonna be the motherfucking teacher!"

Ivery slithered his ass over to me with an evil expression. When he cocked his hand back, I braced my neck for the slap he administered across my cheek.

My eyes shot daggers at him as I stood my ground and showed his weak ass no fear. There was no way that he would get the satisfaction of breaking me down. That just wasn't about to happen.

"Oh, now you aint got shit to say?" Ivery barked as he lifted me off of the concrete floor by my neck.

My feet were dangling and my oxygen was cut off. Ivery didn't give a fuck. Shit, that nigga was still talking mad shit.

"I plan on fucking you up until you bow down as my main bitch! I'm about to blow your back out every chance I get. I'm gonna fuck you in every hole available and ways you can't even imagine!"

As Ivery loosened his hold, my body hit the floor hard. My hands were tied behind me so there was no way that I could brace myself for the fall. He then turned around to face Rick.

"Now as for you, Nigga don't ever question me about how I run my shit! That hot one I grazed you with should have shown you that I don't play. I could have easily killed your ass that night!"

Rick didn't say shit. He just stood there like a damn flunky and nodded to everything that Ivery said. Now Sydney, he was standing over in the cut as if he was plotting something. I didn't know what it was, but his ass was looking sneaky as hell.

"Rick, go get some bedding and shit to bring out here!" Ivery demanded as he tossed him a grip of cash. "I can't be tearing that pussy up on no damn concrete floor."

Grabbing his dick through his pants, Ivery stroked it up and down as he bit down on his bottom lip and smiled. Yes, he was a devious motherfucker but he was going to get back everything he had ever done to me, and then some. If I couldn't get to him, I knew that Trent would.

"I'll be back for your ass too," he whispered as he bent down and licked the side of my face.

"Fuck you, ol' dick in the booty ass bastard!" I chanted in my mind as I cut my eyes at him and clinched my teeth tightly.

"Sydney, take this bitch in the other room and wash her ass up! I want my pussy fresh and clean, clean!" Ivery grinned as he stepped to his nephew and snatched him up by his shirt.

"I'm out of here for a minute. Since I have to go and finish that pig off. I can't send you to do nothing! Why couldn't you just kill that nigga Trent like I did that bitch Kelsie?"

Hearing Ivery admit that he took my best friends life sent chills up my spine and brought anger into my heart. He was a reckless, selfish, snake bastard that didn't give a damn who he hurt. First Kingsman, now Ivery was with the fuck shit.

Kelsie may have had gotten caught up in some bullshit and made some bad decisions, but she didn't deserve to be killed like that. He had beaten the shit out of her to the point that she could barely be recognized.

"If he thinks I'm gonna let him do that to me that nigga is crazy!" I fussed silently as I planned his demise. "I'm gonna play his game and catch him slipping. When I do, his ass is gonna fucking pay especially for Kelsie!"

Within minutes, Ivery and Rick were gone and that left me alone with Sydney. He wasted no time to help me to my feet and escort me to a small room that was just a few feet away. It contained nothing but an open shower, sink and a toilet.

Saying not a word, Sydney started the water and began to undress me. When he got me down to my bra and panties, he paused and stared at my body.

I could see the lust in his eyes as he removed my bra and released my large perky breasts. The coldness in the room made my nipples instantly pop to attention.

"Damn, you're beautiful!" Sydney whispered as he bent down to slide my panties to my ankles and took them off.

I didn't respond in fear of saying the wrong thing. I needed him relaxed enough for me to make an escape.

"Let me bandage your wound before I put you in the water." Sydney informed me before he reached under the sink and drew out a small clear case with a large red cross on the front.

He opened it up and took a wipe out and cleaned the deep cut I had on my side without taking the ties off of my wrists. As soon as he touched the wet alcohol solution onto my wound I gasped out in pain.

"I'm sorry Dylasia," he apologized sincerely. "I didn't mean to drag you through those rocks but I had to get you to Ivery before he killed my mother."

"Huh?" I spoke my first words.

"Yeah, I got mixed up with my father's brother a few years ago. The money was so good that I couldn't get out of the game." Sydney explained as he guided me under the water and began washing me up. "Next he got me strung on drugs and from then on I barely stayed sober. I really didn't think it was that bad until that nigga started doing grimey shit to the women. After that, I told him I wanted out. I guess he was so worried about me telling on him that he started fucking my mother to make sure I didn't go to the police!"

"What? Where's your father?" I asked curiously. "He just let that shit happen? He just let his brother fuck his wife?"

"That's the fucked up thing," Sydney went on. "My father has been missing since last year. Right before Ivery started giving my mother drugs and sexually abusing her."

"Why didn't you do something?"

Sydney's head rose and he looked me in the face. "Because..."

The shame in his eyes told me that he had done something that was too bad to share. I didn't care though. I pressed his ass until he spilled the fucking beans.

"He's done things to me that..."

"What? What did he do to you?"

"Nothing, he just has my head so fucked up that I don't know who I am anymore." Sydney admitted through watery eyes. "When I was just a teenager he held a gun to my head and made me... he made me..."

"What? He made you do what Sydney?"

Clamming completely up, he turned off the water and grabbed the large beach towel and wrapped it around me. He then led me back to the large room and sat me in a metal chair with a leather padded seat. I couldn't even lean back because of the way my hands were still tied behind my back.

Seeing that I was very uncomfortable, instead of binding me to the chair Sydney left me sitting there. He then walked over to the wall and sat on the floor. He put his head in his hands and began to get upset.

It was now or never, I had to take my chances. "Let me tell you something Sydney," I began. "My mother had a terrible drug habit. It started when I was a kid. At first it wasn't that bad, but then she began letting men and women sexually molest me. That shit still kills my soul to this day."

I explained in detail all the horrible things that I had experienced as a young girl. The memories still hurt but as I told Sydney about them I was somehow getting a release from it.

"Are you serious?" Sydney gasped as he came over to me to hug me.

"Yes, I am. If it wasn't for my grandmother there's no telling where I'd be."

I made sure to be as sincere as possible. One wrong move and I could be back tied the fuck up to the chair.

When he let me go, he began to tell me all the unforgivable shit that Ivery had done to him and his mother. "If he didn't have a woman for the night, he would make me suck his dick before he went to bed. Then he made me sleep on the floor and as soon as he woke up with a hard on I had to take care of it. Soon as he got done I had to leave the room right away and send my mother in. If he wasn't in the mood for her, it was my ass that he would take."

"How old were you when it started?" I asked with my mouth still dangling open.

"The first time I gave him head I was seven. I remember he put on a porno and stroked his dick like the guy on the movie. When it got big he told me to suck it like a popsicle. He told me the better I did it the more rewards I would get."

The confession was filled with so much sickness that I nearly threw up. That man needed to die, not go to jail.

It just made me want to kill Ivery even more. Not for me, but for Kelsie and Sydney. They got it way worse than I did.

"Ivery gotta go!" I blurted out right before we saw Rick come in dragging some mattresses. He brought in some fruity ass nigga with him. That nigga was looking real suspect.

Rick gave us the side eye before Sydney hopped up like we had been doing something wrong. I cut my eyes at him.

"Where you want this boo?" the guy asked.

"Didn't I tell you don't be calling me that shit nigga?" Rick hushed him up by knocking him the fuck out right where he once stood. Then he turned to Sydney. "Syd, set the shit up! I gotta go!"

Rick stomped on his way out while the little bitch made nigga hurried up flew his ass up out of there behind him. I could see the embarrassment on his face. Yeah, his ass should've been shame.

Once they were out of sight, Sydney checked on my cut. It had completely soaked the bandage and was dripping down onto the floor.

"I can't stop this bleeding. I'm gonna have to take you and drop you off at the hospital," he told me as he helped me to my feet after removing the loose ties that were around my ankles.

"What are you gonna tell Ivery?" I questioned as we headed toward the exit door and out to his car.

"I'll figure all that out later." Sydney smirked. "Right now I want to drop you off and go check on my mother. Our talk just made me realize that it's not too late. My mom is still alive. Maybe I can still save her."

Sydney's intentions were heartfelt and I wished him the best, but before I could tell him I became dizzy and nauseous. "Ugh"

My hands and legs grew still and I could barely feel them. Next thing I knew my body began to shake uncontrollably. I was going into shock...

Chapter 2

"Agent Santiago, did you hear me?" The raspy voice startled me.

I heard the constant beeping of what sounded like a heart monitor. I fully opened my eyes and scanned the room.

"Where the hell am I?" I quizzed staring up at Trent sitting in a wheelchair and some strange man standing beside him. For a second I almost forgot his last name was Santiago.

"I'm Agent Malcolm Holmes and you are in Kindred Hospital. We got an alert from your home and found Agent Santiago shot. He was able to tell us that someone took you. Right away we activated the tracker that was placed in your pocket before you were removed from your house. You have Agent Santiago to thank for that one. Well, once we got to the location where you were being held, you were being put in a car. That's when we were able to follow you here." Agent Holmes explained.

"I had started this mission to bring down a criminal sex ring but this is deeper than I ever anticipated. No need to worry though, Ivery and everyone else responsible for the havoc will get the maximum consequences."

I was still feeling a bit confused. I just had to ask again how Trent was able to put a tracking device on me. With all that was going on I could hardly remember anything that happened. Only bits and pieces…

"I was actually bringing down the tracker to show you when I saw that same dude that was with Ivery on the video! I watched him creep to the front door on my security monitor as I yelled out to you." Trent verbally recalled as he wheeled near my bed. "Everything happened so fast. All I knew was that I had to get that tracker on you!"

As I responded to Trent, I remembered him being shot. "Are you okay, baby? I thought I was going…"

"Don't speak those words ever. I'm good. One of the bullets just grazed me and the other one they were able to remove with a minor surgery. They just put me in this fucking chair talking about some damn hospital procedures. The hell with this shit! I need to find this Ivery cat before anything else drastic happens!"

As we spoke, several doctors came into the room. While two came to check my vitals, one went to see about Trent.

"Ma'am, we're going to have to keep you here for 24 hours while we monitor you and run some additional tests."

"Well I guess both of you are stuck in here until tomorrow," Agent Holmes chuckled as he stuck his pen and small tablet inside his jacket pocket. "I will have men posted up at every entrance and exit until you two are discharged."

"I appreciate you man." Trent thanked his partner.

"Are you ready for me to wheel you back to your room?" One of the doctors asked Trent.

"No, I'm staying right here with my girl and I don't want to hear shit about hospital rules! Either you get another bed up in here or have me sue you for any and everything I can come up with!" Trent snapped. "Trust I have the best BCA lawyer's on speed dial!"

Agent Holmes laughed before leaving out the door. "I think you better listen to the man. His reach extends pretty far up at the Bureau!"

Both the physicians glanced at one another and then back at Trent. Right away they told him that they would move us to a bigger room so that we could stay together. That was all we wanted…

****

We gave the hospital staff the hardest time for the next twenty-four hours. They were more than ready to get rid of us…

"A car is waiting for you downstairs sir," the nurse informed us as she handed us our discharge papers. "We have to wheel both of you down…"

"Don't tell me! Hospital rules huh?" Trent huffed as he sat his ass right back in the wheelchair and began pouting. "I swear this is some dumb shit!"

The shorter nurse gave Trent a dirty look and I had to chop her ass up! That bitch had been pushing it all morning.

"Look lady, do your job and quit looking at folks all crazy and shit. That's how people get fucked up!" I huffed.

Those two nurses must have wheeled us down to the lobby in record timing. We were sent a personal Town that was waiting in front, courtesy of the Bureau…

Trent gave the driver instructions to take us to his house in the city. We weren't going to the one in Tempe. It had already been compromised.

"How many damn houses do you have?" I huffed feeling left out of the loop. "I told you that you have too many secrets for me!"

"Well, once you marry me then I won't have to keep so many things from you," Trent teased.

"You keep referring to marriage when we just got in a real relationship. Chill yo' ass out!" I retorted keeping Trent on his toes.

He just smiled and shook his head at me.

"So where is this house?" I inquired curiously.

"Dy' you better stop playing with me. You are mines indefinitely, so of course I'm going to talk about our future. And to silence your worries, the house is over on the north side in a new community called 'Rose Garden Lakes'." He answered.

"This is the one that I purchased last year. I have only been there a few times. I wasn't going to stay in it until I retired from this bullshit, but I guess it came in handy now huh."

Trent went on to tell me how he planned on getting out of the Bureau. He had been in there long enough and at thirty he was already in the position to walk away with a healthy bonus. By the way he explained it, he wouldn't have to work another day in his life.

"So what would you do with your time?" I asked.

"I'm gonna open up my own private investigation firm. I'm gonna put your nosey ass on the payroll first!" Trent teased then kissed my cheek. "No but seriously baby. We're gonna start our own business. After this I'm not working for no motherfucker and neither are you, especially that fucking strip club."

"No, I had enough of that shit!" I answered honestly.

I was beyond done especially after I found out about Rick...

Chapter 3

Although both Trent and I were slightly injured, we still found the strength to wrap up in one another's arms. There, I felt safer than anywhere I had ever been in my life. Just like before. We would be the prey.

I hated feeling trapped and having to watch over my shoulders. Hell I hadn't done anything to anyone. Motherfuckers wanted my goodies for profit and I wasn't having that shit.

Rolling over on my stomach I stared into Trent's eyes and told him what happened when I was with Sydney.

"Please, don't tell me you are feeling sorry for this piece of shit after he damn near killed us? I tried to play nice with that fuck boy and do my job, now the gloves gotta come off. Then to find out all along this nigga is a closet dick sucker?" Trent scoffed with his veins popping out.

"I mean, I do feel bad for Sydney now that I know he was being forced and pimped out too, Trent." I explained solemnly.

"Look, we're about to play their little game with them. I'm afraid if we don't go after them now, Ivery's going to kill Sydney for letting me go. I have enough on my conscious already baby." I traced my fingers along his chiseled arms.

"Fuck them nigga's Dy' on some real shit! None of this shit would have happened if a motherfucker stayed loyal to you in the first place! Now here we are all bandaged up and wounded because you're too loyal to the next bitch who don't give a fuck about you! Them nigga's can stick a fork in it, they're done." Trent stood up out of the bed slipping on his boxers.

"Where are you going Trent?" I asked slightly annoyed.

"To hunt."

I slid the covers back quickly and got dressed right with him. I understood why he was mad at me, but I cared for others by default and maybe I did need to fall back some.

Once I finished getting ready I left out the master bedroom behind him. I was going whether he approved or not.

Trent strolled down the long corridor until he unlocked another door. Inside he opened up a huge wall safe and removed several guns, boxes of bullets, two bullet proof vests that read FBI on the front, a set of disposable phones, and some night vision heat sensor goggles. That nigga was suiting up for war and I instantly became worried.

"Catch baby!" Tossing me a set of car keys Trent lifted the garage door from a touch screen monitor. I was in awe and his intelligence was so damn sexy.

Walking up to Trent I placed my hand on the back of his head and leaned in welcoming his cool minty breath as my lips invaded his. The intensity from our passionate kiss left me speechless as I watched him lock everything up before we left out. His mysterious no non-sense demeanor was one of the reasons I was more mesmerized by his calmness.

"The club closes at 3 a.m. so we are going to wait until then to go after Rick first. You think he's still doing shit the same or do you think he switched up after all the bullshit?" Trent interrogated me while intertwining our fingers.

"Remember the last time we snuck up in there? We should go just a little earlier. You know we almost got caught that time!" I replied.

I knew everyone's business in that shady ass establishment, yet I kept my lips sealed. As long as I got my money, what the hell did I care if Rick was running bitches out of the club for Ivery? It didn't matter until they just had to come for me.

Just thinking about how many other people's lives that nigga Ivery had destroyed, I got sick to my stomach. I respected nobody that could do such things…

Placing the camouflage duffle bag inside the back seat of the car, Trent opened the driver side of the door for me. I climbed in while he just stood there with his eyes glued to me.

"Why are you giving me the look?" I asked him as I fastened my seatbelt. He was watching me intensely and it was sending chills up my spine. It was like he was staring at my soul.

"The twinkle in your eyes has changed, so has your posture. You're uptight and scared. There's no need to be." Trent spoke while gazing at me powerfully. He then drew my hand up to his mouth and kissed the tip of my fingers.

Damn, that nigga read me like he was Miss Cleo's little brother and shit. I shook my head and smiled as I revved the engine and brought the silver Impala to life.

Trent made his way around to his side and slid into his whip. It was like I was his Bonnie and he was my Clyde. We made a great team and an even greater couple.

"He truly is my Knight in shining armor..."

Chapter 4

Trent and I arrived at the club a quarter after two, which for Rick use to be his money hour when Kelsie and I performed our solo sets. Not anymore though. The females that still worked there were good but not as good as us. Fuck that shit!

Parking near a SUV, and a few other cars to blend in with, I cut off the engine. Suddenly, Trent had become eerily quiet as we sat and watched the club. The buzzing of his phone served as a quick distraction. Trent answered.

"What's going on Malcolm?" He asked keeping his eyes locked on the entrance to the club.

"We found the building where they were holding your girl. This is a known stash spot of theirs where they keep the women until they can start working." Agent Malcolm informed Trent.

"So were there any casualties on the scene?" Trent questioned Agent Malcolm. I sat listening to everything they were discussing because he placed the speakerphone on.

"No there wasn't, but we did find a pool of blood near an empty chair with broken twist ties, and bloody rags in a bathroom. Other than that we're still following the trail." Malcolm replied pausing to give instructions to an officer.

"Well I'm staking out the second target's establishment as we speak and we have company. Let me call you back!" Trent rushed ending the call abruptly.

Tossing the phone into his snap pocket, he removed the vest from the back seat handing me one. "Put this on." Trent ordered.

I did as I was told as he loaded the clips into his .45 police special twin Glocks placing them in their holsters.

"Take this, it has safety bullets but there will be enough force on impact to knock a bear down. I don't give a fuck what's going on aim and shoot."

Gripping the 9mm gun in my hands, I saw a reflection of Ivery and Desire coming out of the club. I nudged Trent in his side.

"This was the same act he used to try and persuade you that night he approached you." Trent stated.

I turned my nose up at him, because how the hell did he know what took place with Ivery and I the night I was in the car with him. What was really going on?

"How long have you been following and watching me!" I barked feeling on edge with his news.

"It doesn't matter now Dylasia, I'm just glad that I was because look what could have happened." Trent retorted not taking his eyes off of Ivery.

I was more heated than a motherfucker. It was now starting to all make sense to me. Trent was investigating Rick, Ivery, and Sydney from the beginning. I was starting to feel like an 'incentive fuck' in his investigation.

I remained calm but the revengeful bitch in me was starting to surface. I watched with anger as Ivery and Desire sat in his Maybach for a moment. Suddenly, an idea surfaced. I hurried up and shared it with Trent.

"This is Agent Santiago requesting a tail on license number AZ Q as in Quantico, L as in Larry, R as in Rick 314XT, gold luxury Maybach sedan." Trent spoke into the radio receiver underneath the dash. I hadn't even paid any attention to the device until then.

"Trent, call Malcolm back!" I shouted easing out of the car then walking swiftly towards the back of the club near the exit.

I could hear Trent shouting curse words at me and at that point I didn't give a care anymore. They were about to see a side of this desert chick they weren't ready for. I removed the gun Trent gave me checking to make sure the safety wasn't on.

Crouching up against the brick building, I waited for Dex, the head of security to do his rounds while he locked up. Strapping the bullet proof vest up tightly, I sat waiting.

All parties involved were about to feel my fury since they all played on me being a down, real ass bitch. It was now the Dylasia show...

Chapter 5

"Get your ass over here now Malcolm! Our target is with a new girl as we speak and Dylasia has gone inside the club after the owner Rick. I put a tail on that numb nut. I'm heading in behind Dylasia." Trent huffed glaring at me as he caught his breath before hanging up on Agent Malcolm.

"All clear in the back, boss!" Dex shouted placing a brick in between the door to keep it from closing. I watched as he began tossing the black trash bags in the dumpster. He was clueless that we were right on his ass.

I didn't wait another second or look for Trent to take the lead. "Nigga, make one sound and

I'll end your career right here. Move!" I barked at Dex aiming the gun at his temple.

Trent was now standing in front of us to make sure that there was no one coming. Next, I pushed Dex forward so he could see my face. The expression on his was priceless.

"When I ask you a question, you just nod your head yes or no. Is Rick in his office alone?" I grilled him. Dex nodded his head side to side, letting me know Rick had company.

"Are they dancers?" Dex nodded his head up and down shifting his eyes over to Trent who was adjusting the twist ties.

Dex was a big dude standing 6'2, weighing at least three hundred and fifty pounds give or take. Hell, from the way he was sizing Trent up I knew that the situation could get ugly at any moment. I clenched the pistol tightly in my hands before slapping Dex upside the back of his head with it.

Unexpectedly, the gun went off as Dex fell onto the ground making a loud thumping sound. Trent hurried and tied him up.

"Fuck him! Let's go before Rick or someone else comes out." I whispered to him while creeping inside the club.

When we got to the office door, we listened closely. All we could hear was Rick moaning over some softly playing music.

"Aint this a bitch!" I whispered not wanting to walk in on nobody's ass up in the air. I wasn't ready to see no shit like that, especially if it was Rick's overweight ass.

"Let's go in. I need those files and him in custody tonight!" Trent spoke in a low tone as he was about to twist the knob to go in.

"If we bust in right now and get everything, Ivery will be on to us and he'll skip town," I warned becoming a little worried about Ivery still being on the loose. I didn't feel like continuing to run from his punk ass. I was still a liability to him, therefore I would always be in danger until he was behind bars or in the ground becoming maggot food. Either way the shit had to end.

"The shit we took last time wasn't enough to tie Ivery to a damn thing. We need something solid to put him away."

"Do you know for sure if the documents are inside?" I double checked as I held on to Trent's wrist to prevent him from entering.

"Why are you hesitating now Dy?"

"Something just feels off. Something isn't right." I blurted out without realizing what I was saying. I didn't feel that way until that very second.

"Where that nigga at?" Ivery said from afar. He wasn't in plain view just yet, but by his footsteps growing louder I had a good idea that he was on his way towards us.

Trent snatched me up off of my feet and placed me back into a small space between the wall and hallway window. There wasn't enough room for Trent. All he could do was lower his hat and act like he was staring outside.

"What the fuck you doing up here yo? The club is closed." Ivery barked with Desire on his arm. She held on to him and giggled.

"Leave him alone. He's probably just waiting on Rick." Desire laughed.

"Well he's gonna be tied up for a minute so why don't you come back later?"

"Why don't you just get the fuck in there with ya buddy so I can bust both of you sorry motherfuckers!" Trent barked as he pulled his weapon and held it on Ivery and Desire.

That punk bitch nigga tried to make a break for it, but Malcolm and his backup were right there to stop him. I was so glad because I thought we were about to have a damn shootout. In that little ass space we all would have been fucked up.

I guess Rick and the two bitches he had up in there didn't hear shit. He couldn't have because he was too busy getting his dick sucked by one chick while the other was eating her pussy. They didn't stop until Trent turned the music off.

"What the fuck?" Rick shouted as he pulled his dick out and shot his semen all over the chick and Malcolm who was standing near ready to handcuff him.

"Motherfucker!" Malcolm yelled as he cracked Rick in the head. "You nasty bastard!"

He walked over into the private bathroom in Rick's office to clean up. Trent made the girls get dressed and sit on one side of the room.

"Cuff them and search the files." Trent ordered while he checked on me.

"I hope you find something. You know after that incident the last time Rick may have moved that shit." I whispered.

Sure enough, after an hour of searching and tearing up the place, Malcolm and his boys turned up with nothing. They couldn't even get Rick on any minor club violations. They had no choice but to let them go.

"Are you fucking kidding?" I hollered. "You're letting them leave? You have the tapes and everything and that's not enough?"

"The tapes aren't admissible because we didn't have a warrant to place them there. They aren't clear enough even with enhancements. We can't properly identify Ivery or Rick in any of them." Trent sighed looking defeated.

"So what now, I'm still on the run?" I cried. "You know that fool is gonna come straight for me!"

As I said that I watched Malcolm take the cuffs off of Ivery. I looked up until we made eye contact.

"You're fucking dead!" he mouthed before he turned to walk away.

I knew he meant that shit too. That was okay because I was going to get his ass before he even thought about getting me…

Chapter 6

That night we went back to Trent's secret spot. That was the only place I felt safe right then.

"Are you okay?" he asked as he poured me a drink and handed it to me.

Stepping outside the family room sliding doors, Trent hit the power switch on the Jacuzzi and lit some candles.

It was now after five in the morning and I knew the sun would be coming up soon. My days and nights were so mixed up lately that I barely knew when I was coming and going.

"Come outside with me so you can relax baby," Trent suggested as he stood in the doorway and held his hand out to me.

I got up and followed him out. "Can you turn some music on baby?"

While Trent went over to the other side of the deck, I quickly slid out of all my clothes. "Whooo it's cold!"

"Damn, no wonder!" Trent gasped while his eyes got stuck on my private parts.

"No wonder what?" I giggled as I slipped into the warm bubbly water and partially submerged myself.

"Naw, I was just teasing because I didn't expect to see you get naked so fast," he laughed as he got undressed and joined me.

"You already know baby," I smiled while reaching for my drink that I had setting on the table beside the hot tub.

Suddenly an owl swooped down and landed on the nearby brick wall. It was a greyish white color and it was so beautiful.

"I never see them out where I live," I gasped as I stared at it. I was truly amazed.

"Yeah, they come out at this time pretty often," Trent said as if it wasn't a big deal.

Before long, it spread its wide wings and flew off into the darkness.

"That was so tight!" I repeated. "I should've gotten a picture of it!"

Reaching over to me, Trent began massaging my shoulders totally distracting me from enjoying the nature. I tried to appreciate it but my mind kept shifting back to the many questions I had about his work and his intentions with me. I couldn't help but to think that I was just a pawn in his plan to bring down Ivery the whole time.

"What is it Dy?"

"Nothing…"

"Don't tell me nothing when I can feel how tense you are," Trent sighed as he put more pressure into rubbing my back and shoulders.

Turning to him, I began to speak but when I opened my mouth he filled it with his warm sweet tongue. He swirled it around as his soft lips pressed against mine. "Damn!"

Using his hands he caressed my breasts, taking one in each palm. It was feeling so good.

"Oh, my, oh, shit…" I whispered as I felt my body temperature rise.

As the sweat cascaded down my forehead, I held my head back to stop it from dripping into my eyes. Trent took that as an opportunity to kiss my neck and move a little closer.

Taking his hand off only my right breast, he moved it below to finger me nicely. The stimulation between to two had me moaning and grinding up against his hand until I screamed his name and released my first orgasm. That shit made me so horny that I was dragging Trent's ass out of the hot tub and into the house. We couldn't even make it to his bedroom. We made love right there on the floor in the family room. We didn't stop until neither one of us could breathe. That was just what I wanted because right afterwards I passed the hell out. We both did. Right there on the plush carpet in front of the sofa…

****

The peaceful sleep lasted all of three hours. That was when the alarm went off and had us both damn near jumping out of our skin.

"Stay right here!" Trent ordered as he hopped up with his dick just a swinging. I was scared but at the same time I couldn't help but laugh.

Scrambling to my feet, I tried to find something to cover up with. By the time I did, it was too late. Malcolm was standing right there with his eyes about to buck out of his fucking face.

"Man, pick ya lip up!" Trent huffed while he stood in front of me to block Malcolm's view just long enough for me to slide my shirt up over my head.

I rushed out of the room and gave them some privacy. Plus, I had to get somewhere and find something to put on. That shit right there was fucking embarrassing…

Once I found some gym shorts, I eased back through the kitchen and paused at the doorway to the family room. I could hear Malcolm and Trent talking.

"You know we done fucked up now right?" Malcolm whispered.

"Maybe not," Trent hushed him up. "Dy doesn't know everything."

"Does she know that you're married?"

I jumped to attention and wound up knocking the cordless phone off of the kitchen counter. That caused all the attention to shift towards me.

"Okay man," Malcolm said as he dapped up Trent. "I'll call you this afternoon, and sorry about tripping your alarm. I didn't know that shit was that sensitive."

The minute Malcolm left, Trent asked me how much of the conversation did I hear. I was truthful with him and I was damn sure hurt.

Before I could start questioning him, tears ran down my face. I didn't even know what to ask first.

"Damn," I sniffled.

While I tried to pull it together, Trent walked off and came right back holding some documents. He didn't explain. He just let me read them.

I took the papers from him and sat on the sofa then turned on a nearby lamp so that I could see clearly. Slowly scanning them, I saw that he was indeed married and his wife was dead. She was murdered. All the evidence traced back to a sex ring.

"Was Ivery behind this?" I questioned hesitantly.

"No, I think his father was…"

Wow, the shit was way deeper than I ever imagined. I had to know the details…

Chapter 7

Sitting on the couch reading over Trent's wife's case file, a bitch was more than shook. Quite a few of Ivery's family members were known human sex traffickers. His father was number four on the Bureau's top ten most wanted list, and well beyond dangerous.

Looking up into Trent's warm eyes, I could see the anguish clear as day. "Please, don't lie to me. Did you pursue me in order to build a case that would put Ivery's family away?" I asked already knowing the answer. I just needed to hear Trent admit it.

He sighed heavily taking my hand in his. "I've never lied to you so I won't start. Initially you were under investigation as well just because you worked at the strip club. Kelsie, Ivery, Sydney, along with Rick were prime suspects but after constant surveillance I removed you as apart of the sex ring. I realized that you didn't know Ivery until the night of his party at the club."

"So you purposely used me? Trent, do you understand that motherfuckers like Ivery and his father don't care about casualties? Look what happened to your wife! Look what happened to Kelsie! They've already came after us twice. I was so fucking stupid, all this time I thought what we had some real thug loving here!" I huffed getting up off the couch. "I was way off! Shit you a thug with a badge that just looks at me like another stripper chick huh?"

"I'm not even gonna justify that shit with an answer Dy," Trent sighed before kissing me in my mouth. "I'm passed all the bullshit. I don't care how the shit started. I love you now and I'm not gonna let what happened to my wife happen to you. You mean way too much to me baby."

I listened to Trent, but my mind kept shifting back to his wife. I couldn't believe he didn't tell me about her. That shit made me feel some type of way.

Glancing down at the array of crime scene photographs, Trent's wife's murder hung over me like a plague. She was beautiful and so young, but Trent couldn't save her so how the hell could he and the bureau save me?

"Listen Dylasia, there was no way to know I'd fall in love with you. Now my only mission is to make those responsible for my wife's murder pay and at the same time protect the woman who has given me another chance at love. I apologize for not being up front with you but my job is to investigate." Trent confessed wrapping his arms around my waist tighter.

For a moment, I wanted badly to believe Trent truly cared for me and meant what he said. Thing was, my luck and trust in people I thought I knew showed me otherwise. Plus it was his job to persuade, interrogate, and some more shit. He was good at it too. He surely had my ass fooled.

Trent must have thought his charming smile and strong embrace would calm my fears; wrong. If someone didn't take Ivery out I was going to end up like Trent's wife! "Shit, no not me!" Now, more than ever I had to protect my family. Big Mama was all I had left.

"Oh my God, I've been so caught up in our fake ass fairytale I haven't even checked on my grandmother!" I tore out of Trent's hold and stormed off in a hurry to grab my things.

I felt so bad that I had been ignoring my priorities. Reason being, I was too busy trying to get revenge against those sick twisted fucks while totally forgetting to check on Big Mama.

Gathering what clothes I had to put on, I got dressed in two seconds flat. My car was still parked at Big Mama's. "Shit!" I spat as I remembered then headed back downstairs.

Trent was standing by the door suited and booted with his guns in holster. "Where are you going Dy'?" he quizzed blocking the entrance to the garage.

"Where I should have been in the first place! My mom just got killed and I abandoned the only person I have left in this whole world! Move out of my way!" I shouted.

Trent stood there not budging at all. I turned running towards the front door, but he was on my ass so fast. He immediately began wrestling with me so I wouldn't leave.

"Let me go Trent!" I whined squirming trying to get away but he was too strong. I wasn't ready to give up just yet though.

"Ugh!" I screamed with tears rapidly falling as we fell onto the floor.

"Why are you crying Dy?" Trent asked holding me closely while wiping away the tears from my face.

"Because Trent... All I want is to be happy and successful. I don't bother anyone yet my life is a fucking mess! I fell in love with a fraud who pretended to be interested in me only to close out a big fucking case! My bestfriend and mom are dead. I'm homeless not to mention my job at the newspaper fired me. I just want to be left alone."

"I apologize Dy' for the way the events played out, but nothing is fake about the way I feel for you, and me being here with you. I am madly in love with you and I'm not letting you go for anything or anyone. We can move Big Mama in the morning. Right now, we're going to bed. Try to rest, and we'll start bright and early tomorrow." He replied lifting some of his weight up off me.

It was just enough for me to shake loose. I wasted no time hopping up to my feet.

"Fuck you and them!" I shouted.

Trent thought I was still naive at the situation at hand; not! He needed me to get to Ivery and his father's organization. I had different intentions. I was done being the prey! It was time for me to be the predator.

I stared at Trent shooting daggers with my eyes. He looked right back at me with no fear.

"Take me to my grandmother now or else!..." I snapped removing one of Trent's gun from his holster before he realized what happened.

"Dylasia! Put the fucking gun down now!" Trent barked scaring me just a little at first. I quickly shook that shit off because I wasn't playing and was hardly fazed by his tone.

"Where are the keys to the car? Toss them to me!" I ordered watching him carefully as we walked towards the garage.

Trent handed me the keys as he eyed my every move. I pressed the automatic start button as the engine came to life.

I blew Trent a kiss and ran my ass up outta there faster than a track star competing for a gold medal. Right then I couldn't worry about how Trent felt. I had to go get Big Mama.

Chapter 8

"Big Mama!" I yelled the minute my key opened the door. The house was eerily quiet and that shit put my senses on high alert because my grandma always kept her television on.

Immediately panic started to kick in. I couldn't let it take over. Instead I allowed it to fuel my body to find my grandmother.

I searched her three bedroom house top to bottom but Big Mama wasn't there. "Where the hell is she?"

Walking into her room everything was in place like always. Her bed was made with her praying cloth over her pillow. Then I saw the note on her bible sitting on the night stand.

Picking up the small piece of folded paper, I knew my grandmother had written it. It was definitely her handwriting.

Dy-Dy I prayed to the Good Lord to cover and protect you from worthless pieces of shit but the devil uses everyone he can with sheep's wool. Don't worry about me, I can handle myself. If you're reading this some pretty Toni snake came by telling me I had to go with him because you wouldn't answer his calls.

Something wasn't right about him but I went anyway. He's driving one of those nice foreign cars you see on TV. I tucked my Obama phone in my brassiere in case you call... He's coming back now.

I love you Dylasia..

I read my grandmother words and felt my body fill with so much anger. It was all my fault Big Mama was in harms way in the first place.

"Lord, please protect my Big Mama. I'm going to kill this nigga once and for all! " I ran to my old room removing a pair of black yoga pants, black Cami and changed.

"Whatever you're thinking about doing you'll need my help." The familiar voice spoke from out in the hallway. I was having flashbacks of Kingsman.

I turned around not ready for another unexpected surprise, not thinking twice I squeezed the trigger. "Oh fuck!" Sydney cried out clutching his arm.

I ran to his side feeling bad for shooting him but then again what the fuck was Sydney doing there anyway? I was feeling totally confused.

I stood back up and focused my gun on him once again. "Where is my grandma Sydney?" I grilled him.

"Ivery has her! I was told that if I didn't come back with you, he was going to kill my mom or sell her to the highest bidder." Sydney replied wincing from the pain.

"Oh yeah! Well today is yo lucky day. I'm not about to keep playing hide and seek with this fuck boy. He wants me so bad, take me to him! I tried to be a good girl but now the bad bitch Dy' has pushed through. Get the fuck up!" I snapped. Sydney was looking at me confused.

"Look Dylasia I never wanted to hurt you, Kelsie, or any of the other women. I am a victim too but I'd die to save my mom from Ivery."

The sincerity and previous stories Sydney shared with me got the wheels in my head to plotting. Big Mama always told me the best way to trap a rat was to keep cheese around. And that was exactly what I was to Ivery... A piece of cheese.

"Save that sensitive ass speech for your statement to the police. Right now my only concern is taking this bitch ass nigga Ivery out! Either you rocking with me or I'm gon' roll over yo ass too!" I retorted taking my phone out of my jeans.

I sat on the bed. I couldn't dial Trent fast enough.

"Yes Dylasia." He answered calmly.

"He has her Trent and from what Sydney tells me he's not giving her back... Unless Sydney brings me to him. I'm going to see him but first you need to get Agent Malcolm over here with all those spy gadgets and shit. Oh I shot Sydney too!" I informed him and ended my call.

"So this is what we're going to do Syd." I chuckled feeling devious and in control. Ivery didn't know that a good girl gone bad was about to destroy his entire fucking being. Duck, duck, goose.

Chapter 9

Ring...Ring..."Hello." I answered the unfamiliar number.

"Hey its Agent Malcolm, I'm outside." He notified me. I took one last look at Sydney, he nodded his head giving me the go ahead.

In order for my plan to work Sydney was going to have to testify against Ivery. Which meant he was going to tell Trent and Malcolm whatever they had to know. I stood at the front door waiting on Trent and Malcolm to come inside.

Malcolm entered first carrying a huge metal case with Trent right behind him. Trent looked at me then back at Sydney before punching him in his nose first. Blood spewed out on the wall and chair he was sitting in.

"What the fuck Trent!" I spat.

I was really feeling his tough exterior but I had to focus on the matter at hand. The shit was getting crazy.

"That's for him dragging you out my house and shooting me that night!" He replied with a devilish smirk.

"Sorry about that Sydney." I apologized to him.

"It's cool. I deserved it." Sydney said holding his head back.

I excused myself to go get him a towel. I could over hear Trent interrogating him.

"Who the fuck killed my wife? That's what I want to know?" Trent gritted his teeth.

I peeked around the doorway and saw the spit flying out of his mouth as he badgered Sidney about the murder of his wife. I could tell that he was still torn up about it.

The more he questioned him about it, the more I realized that he was still in love with her. I knew he had to be vexed about it. Honestly, I would have too.

After I had heard enough, I cleared my throat as I walked back into the room. Trent was just wrapping up his interrogation.

"Well, let me take him down to the federal building." Malcolm offered. "I'm gonna get him placed into protective custody until we're able to catch Ivery and his father Senior."

"Aight, keep me posted." Trent sighed before grabbing my hand and leading me out to the car. "You leave your car here and ride with me."

Right then I was more than ready to go back to his house and shower and change. Even though that wasn't going to cleanse my insides…

I felt so dirty from everything that I had been through. I probably needed to go to church and get some spiritual cleansing. Hell, I was willing to try anything.

What I really needed was to find Big Mama. She was a very strong woman so I knew that she was using every trick in the book to stay alive. She and I both knew that we were all that we had. I didn't want to lose her. I just couldn't...

While Trent's phone continued to sound off, I urged him to answer it. I thought it might be some information on my grandmother.

"Hello?"

There was a brief pause before Trent began speaking again. "Where did you say that was?"

Trent signaled me to search the glove box and find something to write on. Once I did, he recited an address to me.

When he hung up I questioned him about it. "Is this where Big Mama is?"

"No, that's where Senior, Ivery's father is. There are men watching the house right now."

"That's what Malcolm told you?" I asked.

"No, that was my boss. He calls the shots."

"So you don't wanna just go over there and bust right in so you can get him?"

"Hell yeah, but I have to wait to get the green light," Trent explained. "My boss won't give me that until tomorrow."

"What's the hold up?" I asked curiously.

"Well his wife and small daughter are with him and he doesn't want to start a war over killing or injuring one of them." Trent smirked. "Even though that motherfucker didn't give a shit about my wife and daughter she was carrying…"

"Wait a minute! What?" I shrieked in disbelief. "You keep dropping shit on me left and right! You didn't tell me that she was pregnant Trent! Your wife was carrying your baby?"

Trent pulled over down the street from the house and put the car in 'park'. He slowly turned to me and told me how his daughter lived for three days. She was premature and her lungs weren't fully developed. My heart went out to him. I knew he had to be devastated…

"I'm so sorry," I sniffled getting caught up in the story.

"So you guys never had kids?"

"Nope, that was the first time I had ever gotten anyone pregnant to be honest." Trent frowned as he moved the stick shift downward until it rested in 'drive'.

We rode those few blocks to the house in silence. I didn't know what Trent was thinking, but I sure couldn't get the vision out of my head of his wife and daughter losing their lives to Ivery and his family. That shit right there just made things that more messed up...

Chapter 10

We got back to the house only to fall into one another's arms again. This time it wasn't passionate. It was more like a release of pain. It felt refreshing.

There was no kissing and hugging. It was only humping, screaming, hair pulling and biting. The shit was so intense that it actually put me to sleep. That right there was definitely a first...

The next morning I woke up sore. Every inch of my body was aching, even my coochie. That motherfucker was throbbing something fierce.

Looking over at Trent, I noticed that he was still knocked out. I didn't disturb him. I just drug myself up out of bed and went to the bathroom to piss.

"Shit," I screamed as the urine burned as it came out. Trent had fucked me so hard that I was raw between my legs.

I wiped very carefully and stepped to the sink to wash my hands. When I finished, I cut off the water and glanced up in the mirror at my naked body.

"Oh my fucking goodness!" I gasped. "You gotta be fucking shitting me right now!"

There were scratches on my arms, bite marks on my breasts and hickey's on various parts of me. I couldn't believe my eyes.

Getting a little closer to the mirror, I stared at my reflection. I looked like what I had been through. But, you know what? I was still there.

Now, I had to focus on staying alive long enough to find my grandmother. I couldn't think about nothing else. I didn't plan on resting until that happened. Afterwards I was going to put Ivery and his family away for good. Whether it be behind bars or underground…

"Dy, you hungry baby?" Trent yelled out from the bedroom calming from my inner rage.

I walked back in there without covering up one bit. I wanted Trent to see just what he had done to me.

"Damn baby!" he gasped putting his hand up to his mouth. "I knew we got rough last night but shit!"

I drew back the covers to join him in the bed. When I did, I saw that Trent was just as damaged as I was; scars and all. "Look at you!"

"Knock, knock, knock,"

Out of the blue someone was pounding at Trent's front door. He went straight for his gun.

"Why don't people call first before coming over?" I huffed.

Trent checked his cell only to find out that it was dead. He tossed it on the bed and went on to the door. Whoever it was out there was still banging away on the door.

"It better be Malcolm!" Trent fussed as I slipped on a tank top and ran behind him with the small deuce-deuce he gave me.

Sure enough it was Trent's partner Malcolm. He was out of breath and fussing all at the same time.

"Damn, I've been calling you on the landline and your cell all morning!" he snapped. "Shit is going down and you are up here…"

Malcolm looked at both Trent and I who were standing there in our underwear. Hell you could see straight through the tank top I had on and my ass was hanging out my thong.

I dashed to the back as I heard Malcolm say he forgot what he was going to say after he saw all the marks on our bodies. I wondered like hell what Trent was going to tell him…

"Dy, Dylasia!" he shouted out loudly like it was an emergency.

I slid into my jeans and flip flops and ran to him. "What is it?"

"They think they know where your grandmother is!" Trent revealed before telling his partner to give us five minutes to get ready.

Malcolm stared me down before leaving. It was like he was trying to read me but I didn't know why. I started to ask Trent but I didn't want him thinking the wrong thing so I saved it for a later time.

Trying to ignore the ill vibes I was getting from Malcolm, I followed Trent to the room to get cleaned up and dressed. It didn't take but a few minutes and then we were ready.

We went to the garage and hopped into Trent's Honda. It was compact but roomy on the inside.

"We're gonna follow Malcolm to the spot. I really didn't want to take you with me but I didn't feel like fighting you. I think that's why that nigga is acting salty. It's whatever though. The most important thing right now is getting your grandmother back safe."

"Awwww," I thought to myself. Trent was actually putting my family in front of his need for revenge. Then again, knowing him he had a plan to get Ivery's dad at the same time. It didn't matter to me as long as I got Big Mama back safely. That was my main concern.

Of course I wanted to catch Ivery and his punk ass daddy. They needed to be locked the fuck up. But, if they harmed one damn hair on my grandmother's head they're gonna wish they were dead...

Chapter 11

Traveling to an address located fifteen minutes outside of Phoenix, I couldn't shake all the evident pieces of the puzzle. At first, I was so caught up in the dick down sessions Trent provided that I forgot to find out who the hell I was truly dealing with. I gave him the side eye when my phone chimed blaring out *gospel* music.

Searching around frantically, I found my phone and immediately answered it.

"Big Mama?" I asked on edge. Trent glanced at me then back on the road.

"I don't got long baby." She whispered.

"I know where I'm at but its bad dealings in here. There are some fine young tenders with big guns guarding the rooms. I just acted like I was having a stroke. They went to get me something to eat and drink so I can take my blood pressure medication. Where is Trent? Get y'all ass over here. Address is 176..." Big Mama rattled off before her line went dead.

I could hear chatter in the background but couldn't make out what they were saying. "Fuck!" I spat.

"What did Big Mama say?" Trent asked.

"She was trying to tell me where she was and something about men and guns." I replied giving him partial facts.

"Let me tell Malcolm." Trent said reaching for his phone. I grabbed his hand.

"No you're not going to tell Malcolm shit! Something about this whole situation is wrong." I snapped looking out the windows. There were two black Yukons following us with Malcolm in front.

Starting to think steps ahead, I downloaded a phone locator app on my phone. After entering the number, the GPS signal started tracking the location of my grandmother Obama phone. I didn't say anything just yet to Trent because something wasn't right. It was time for me to start listening to my intuition.

"What's up Dy' tell me what you thinking?" Trent probed not liking the silent treatment I was giving him at the moment.

The direct tower and address of my grandmother location sat on my phone. It was in the opposite direction that Malcolm was leading us. Something was up and my first thought was to bait Trent. I had to make sure he wasn't in on it too. I was going to wait for his response before I figured out how to move forward with him.

"What's up Dy?" Trent asked again.

"What's up is you need to open your eyes sweetheart. All this time you've been keeping shit from me but the main source connected to you is the key. For now, I'm cool on being intimate with you. I gotta get Dylasia back focused. Not to mention you're still in love with your wife. It's too much to deal with." I turned to face him so I could observe his body language.

When I noticed the veins pulsating in his neck, I could tell I had struck a nerve. Good the old Dylasia was null and void.

"I'm not going to discuss the feelings of my wife right now, but once all of this is over I promise I will explain it to you. At the moment, your detective skills are brewing and I want to center in on that."

"What do you mean?"

"I mean, why do you feel that Malcolm is the missing link to all of this?" Trent grilled me as we merged into the fast lane.

I was impressed by his recover on my little test once again. I truly did fall hard for Trent, but to me it felt all felonious the more I found out about his motives. I wasn't sleep anymore. I was wide awake and my eyes were on everyone.

"Listen to this Trent. How come you've been this close to the people responsible for your wife's murder, a multimillion dollar human sex ring, tax invasion, larceny, and too many other facts to name to end this mayhem, but you can't catch them?" I countered.

Instead of answering, Trent seemed to be in deep thought. I didn't give him much time before I was at him again.

"I mean Malcolm was on the case originally right? Corruption is evident right? Plus, how did Ivery know to send Sydney to your place in Tempe? We need to know who Senior and Ivery's source is?" I quizzed laying out all the cards for him.

Trent remained quiet as he continued to process all the information I threw his way. While he continued to think, his eyes scanned the rearview mirror. By the way he adjusted his posture he had to notice the trucks following us as well.

"What happens to a witness that goes into custody?" I asked curiously remembering how Malcolm was so eagered to haul Sydney into custody.

"Once interviewed, we have witnesses sign a sworn statement with the District Attorney present. After that, we relocate the witness safely until trial is done." Trent answered switching lanes before suddenly getting off at the next exit.

I sat up turning slightly to see where the trucks had gone. There was no way that I could tell with the heavy flow of oncoming traffic.

"Why did you get off?" I asked.

Trent maneuvered through the traffic flow until he spotted a secluded area near a business district right outside of Glendale. Placing the car in park, Trent shut the engine off. He got out the car and bent down to look under the body of the car as well as the bumpers. When he got back inside the vehicle, he scanned the interior and in no time he discovered tracking device located underneath the steering wheel. He removed it quickly and tossed it out.

"Dylasia, I trust you with my life and if you are telling me to consider the closest source to me then I'm going to listen."

Trent's eyebrows rose and he began to grit his teeth. I could tell he was bothered.

"I'm calling into the bureau now, if Malcolm is the leak or shady in anyway, I have to protect us first." Trent informed opening the glovebox removing a disposable cell phone.

I sat by watching him closely all the while I was texting Big Mama's phone. I didn't take my eyes off of him for a second. I observed him very closely.

Trent punched a code into the phone, the phone lit up, he then placed a tiny chip on the side.

"This is Agent Trenton Santiago, I'm off the grid but I need the status agents assigned to the Sydney Filmore case." He requested surveying the crowded parking lot.

"I see..." Trent scoffed listening carefully. "Well do me a favor Agent Carlisle, send me a secure location for central Phoenix. One more thing put the bureau on alert with IAB, we have a inside compromising source. I'll check in for a briefing at the safe spot." Trent informed his superiors as he ended the call.

Trent was appearing to transform right before me. His eyes grew darker and his jaw muscles twitched as he hopped out of the car again.

"What is it Trent?" I asked rushing out of the car to his side.

He looked down at me then started stomping on the disposable phone. "Sydney never made it to protective custody and Malcolm hasn't reported in the last two weeks nor has he requested the warrants for Senior and Ivery's arrest." Trent said removing his holster.

"We gotta get your grandmother now and I know exactly how to lure everyone together." He replied sneakily.

"I'm sick of this bureaucratic protocol shit. Get all the guns together and get in! I know where Big Mama is." I snapped tossing him my phone.

"See that's why I love you, proactive and on point!" Trent smiled slapping me on my ass playfully.

I couldn't figure it out, but like my mama used to tell me, '*sometimes following your heart means losing your mind.*'

Chapter 12

Maneuvering through the congestion of rush hour traffic, Trent was rambling on and on about how blind he was to the fact that Malcolm was involved. He kept saying how stupid he felt.

I couldn't console him while he was driving. Plus, the specifics of Trent's wife involvement still bothered me.

"Baby, don't be offended but what was your wife doing associating with people like Ivery's family?" I questioned him curiously.

"Lo... Lorraine was a field agent. She, Malcolm and I met after a long extensive weapons training in. D.C. Occasionally Lorraine and I would work together on high profile assignments during which time we got rather close and started seeing each other outside of the office. After three years of dating, Lorraine and I finally decided to tie the knot even though our work schedules conflicted most of the time."

"So how did you guys see each other? Did you even live together?"

"Well, we flew out to each other when need be..." Trent said becoming emotional. "We owned a house together, but we never got a chance to share it."

"Damn, that's messed up," I sighed.

"Anyway, one morning after I had been granted a Level 5 security clearance, I was also chosen as the lead agent for a special crime task force to bring down the Sonoita Cartel. Came to find out, we were both assigned to the case by two different departments. Lorraine wasn't even supposed to be on field duty because of her pregnancy. She had been on desk detail. When they found out they called us in to reassign us so there wouldn't be any problems. Well, when

Lorraine and I both went to report in that day, Lorraine didn't show up. Instead she was pulled into a private human sex auction. It was discovered by undercover agents when someone recognized Lorraine's little sister, Lorreal, was being auctioned off by Senior. That was her real interest on the case. Nothing could stop her from trying to save her sister. Not even her carrying my baby..." Trent informed me as the GPS locator started buzzing alerting us we were near our location.

"Lorraine was a natural born lioness when those she loved were in danger."

"Well what happened?" I asked.

"Later on that day that she was supposed to show up at the bureau, we found her in front of the police station dead in a state vehicle. Immediately after that, I was temporarily taken off the case but got back on shortly after."

"How did you get back on the case?"

"Once they saw that I wasn't backing off they had no choice but to bring me back on." Trent explained right before the sudden unexpected interruption.

Boom, boom, boom! I heard a loud cannon like sound come from the house. That shit pulled me upright and at attention. Trent too...

Trent jerked me enough for me to shift my position behind the lemon tree just in time to see Ivery crouching down beside his father. Our eyes followed him to the idled truck parked in front of the house.

Soon as they pulled off, we made a beeline back to the car. I didn't want them to get away! I wanted to get Ivery so damn bad and after hearing the facts of Trent's wife's murder, it fueled my adrenaline even more to take his ass out! Both him and his taco eating ass daddy for that matter...

Instead of following when we pulled off, Trent had another idea. He wanted to case the surroundings before making his move. He told me that a flawless strategy required planning in order to execute it properly. I didn't agree with him. I thought we should just chase them down and kill both the bastards' right there in cold blood.

Trent started out by circling the area a few times to find out the best option to take when we went back to Ivery's father's house. I was starting to get impatient.

To distract myself, I glared at all the houses as we drove by. I was in total awe of the luxury miniature mansions.

Now that was more of my style of living. The huge freshly manicured lawns, palm trees, and cactus that sat perfectly along the different homes, it was all beautiful.

"I'm gonna pull right here." Trent found a vacant house in the gorgeous subdivision right on the backside of Senior's house and parked.

We got out, walked to the side of the two-story dwelling, opened the gate and went in the back. There we found an outside staircase with a wooden rail so we crept up in order not to be seen over Senior's fence. "Bingo!" We had a clear view to his backyard.

"Look Trent! It's Malcolm..." I whispered while pointing to the small cottage that sat in the back of Senior's property. "Why hasn't he even called you? I would think he would be blowing your phone up once we stopped following him like we were supposed to!"

"I stomped the cell out remember?" he whispered sounding irritated.

"Oh yeah…"

"Shhhhh," Trent hushed me as he pointed to the inside of the main house. There was an older woman in the kitchen cooking.

My focus went back to Malcolm, who was now pulling out a key and using it to go into the cottage. I couldn't believe the shit.

"What the hell is really going on? I wonder if Big Mama is in there." I thought silently.

Trent and I looked at each other and then back to Ivery's father's property. There were plenty of hiding places in his backyard, but our timing would have to be perfect to execute that shit.

Grabbing me by the hand, Trent led me down the stairs and back to the car. When we drove off I began to question him.

"Are you trying to get these motherfuckers locked up or are we gonna take them out?" I asked because if my grandmother was up in there, I didn't want to leave there without her.

"I have to at least see if she's in that fucking cottage!" I plotted silently.

Trent thought about it too. I knew because he was real quiet and had that look on his face.

"I'm asking because we're doing all this shit for what?" I snapped. "You don't have enough evidence to take them in and you obviously don't have enough balls to murk them sick fuckers! I have to get to Big Mama. I know she's in that cottage that Malcolm went in. She has to be in there!"

Trent slammed on the breaks and threw the car in park. He eyed me down with a frown and spoke to me firmly.

"Originally I was gonna go the legal way. After shit got hectic and he fucked with you too, yeah, I wanted to kill both of them. Then, for them to kidnap your fucking grandmother! I was ready to go up in there with guns blazing. But now, now that you shined the light on Malcolm, it's much bigger than that. It's way bigger!"

Damn, Trent did have a point. If we murdered Ivery and his father, Malcolm could very well get away with whatever sneaky shit he was doing with them. Plus, Big Mama might get caught in the crossfire. I wanted to get her before we did anything else. I couldn't risk her safety unless someone got in our way. Then they would get it.

"So far the paper trail hasn't led us to Malcolm. That tells me right there that his connections run deep." Trent enlightened me. "He has to have someone up high in his pocket. Someone else is involved."

Shit was getting worse by the day. We had to end the mess and we had to end it soon…

Chapter 13

While we were sitting there on the side of the road, we saw Malcolm pass. Lucky we were down far enough in the dip that he didn't even notice us.

"Dy, you think he saw us?" Trent whispered like the nigga could hear us.

"Naw, but do you think my grandmother is in that cottage?"

"I don't know but let's hurry up and go see." Trent said as he started the car up and headed back to Senior's house.

"If we go over the fence in the back, how the hell we gonna get Big Mama back over?" I questioned as we parked and went back to our spot in backyard of the vacant house.

The second we climbed the stairs, the lights went out in the main house. I was getting more and more anxious just thinking about Ivery, Senior or Malcolm coming back. Even though we were armed, I didn't want any sudden gunfire to erupt while we were trying to get Big Mama out.

"Let's go now!" I whispered.

"You take the car and go out front. I will go over the fence and if your grandmother is in there I will bring her out through the side gate over there." Trent instructed. "Keep ya heater in your lap. You don't know who might creep the hell up. Keep your eyes wide the fuck open Dylasia! Please baby. I don't want anything to happen to you."

Trent's words trailed off as I took off running to the car. I did just as he told me. I drove the car around and parked in the cut where he showed me when we were scoping the place. I hit the engine and the lights and got out. I wanted to be ready just in case some shit jumped off.

After a few minutes, I heard the gate open and that was when the fucking alarm went off. I began to panic as I walked closer to the house.

"Start the fucking car!" I heard Trent yell as he damn near drug Big Mama across the lawn. Shit, she was keeping up though...

I ran to the car and keyed the ignition before peeling out of the gravel. I skid beside them and hopped over into the passenger seat to let Trent drive while my grandmother jumped into the backseat.

"Lord Have Mercy!" Big Mama yelled as she grabbed her chest. "Get us the hell up out of here!"

Getting up on my knees in my seat, I turned all the way around so that I could rub my grandmother's shoulder. "Are you okay Big Mama?"

"Yeah, I'm good now that you guys came and got me. I swear I prayed the whole time that you would come Dylasia. I knew Trent would bring you to find me."

My grandmother was in tears as she continued to thank God for sparing her life once again. She spoke about how she didn't deserve the grace he bestowed upon her.

"Yes you do Big Mama!" I assured. "You deserve it and plus the Lord knew I needed you."

"I need you too Dylasia."

"I'm so sorry Big Mama. It's my fault. I drug you into all this." I cried.

"You battle baby girl, is my battle too. We're family and we are all we got." My grandmother said while drying her tears and patted Trent on the shoulder. "Well, now I guess we got you too baby."

Trent responded with a nod and stayed focused on the road ahead as me and my grandmother continued to sniffle. I took my last piece of tissue and gave it to her before I turned back around. That was when I noticed that we were on the freeway.

We had gotten on the loop 101 heading west towards Surprise. Once we passed Deer Valley, I looked around and got curious.

"Where are we going?"

"We're gonna stay out in Buckeye tonight until I can figure something out. It's equipped with everything we need."

This time it was deep out in the west valley. It was almost two hour drive from where we were coming from. Both my grandmother and I were sleep by the time we got there.

"Where are we?" I yawned.

"This is the only spot that I have that Malcolm doesn't know about. It's on the market to be sold but it has all the 'show' furniture in it. It's gonna have to do until I can come up with something else."

I had a good feeling that the house we were at was the one he told me about. The one that he bought with his late wife but never got a chance to stay in. That was just fine with me as long as we would be able to get a good night sleep without worrying. I really needed that.

"Big Mama, wake up," I said shaking her gently. She didn't move. My heart began to beat faster than it ever had in my life. I couldn't even breathe. "Big Mama?"

"What's wrong?" Trent questioned as he turned the car off, got out and went around to open up my grandmother's door. "Big Mama?"

Trent felt for her pulse. "She's definitely alive." He assured as he placed two fingers on her neck.

"Woooo shit!" Big Mama moaned as she slowly sat up straight. "I'm so exhausted I must've dozed off into a deep one huh?"

I blew a deep sigh of relief and said a quick prayer. I didn't know what I would have done if she died on me like that...

Chapter 14

The moment we stepped foot into the house I started questioning Big Mama about what happened. Ivery was a demented soul and I had to know my grandmother was fine.

Meanwhile, Trent was using a disposable cell to notify his superiors of the sudden turn of events. I tuned out my grandmother and listened intensely as I tried to play it off like I wasn't.

"Big Mama, I'm so sorry I hadn't checked on you sooner."I whined sitting down beside her on the wrap-a-round sectional. She caressed my tresses as she rocked holding me in her arm.

"I'm glad you didn't girl! That Mr. Clean looking thug sat with me until he was convinced you weren't stopping by. He's obsessed with you too baby. What you do to that demon child?" Big Mama chuckled staring at me inquisitively.

"It's a long story. But the main thing is you are okay. Tomorrow, I'm sending you to visit aunt Helen, until I can find us a new house." I told her stretching my legs out.

Big Mama started shaking her head back and forth at the mention of her only sister.

"I am not going all the way to no Oakland California to see that penny of a skeezer! No way... I'm not leaving you again. I'm going to go to the good Lords house and have my prayer warriors lay hands on me. I saw, said, and lusted so much, I gotta get this spirit of mine delivered." Big Mama said fanning herself.

I was laughing so hard and holding my stomach at the same damn time. Big Mama was a nut.

"I love you Big Mama." Giving her a hug I squeezed my grandmother tight as I could.

"I love you too, suga."

"I hope you ladies like take out?" Trent asked when he joined us in the living room.

Big Mama released me and went to Trent. She hugged him tightly then let him go.

"Thank you for protecting the only child I have left. You are a fine man Trent and hopefully you and my baby get it right. From the first day I saw you in my house, I knew Dylasia had found a real man, but until you let go of whatever is keeping you from true happiness, her love and loyalty doesn't belong to you. Come correct or don't come knocking at all." She winked at him.

Trent stood there looking stunned. He didn't say a word but he did nod his head affirmatively.

"Now I'm going to my borrowed room and pray. Come get me when the food is here." Big Mama spoke looking Trent straight in the eyes before kissing him on the cheek and leaving.

That woman wasn't a psychic but she could read you your rights. She was always on point!

I grabbed the remote from off of the coffee table and turned on the TV.

"That woman Big Mama is something else." Trent admitted sitting down next to me.

"Try being raised by her." I retorted while channel surfing.

"Look Dy', the card Malcolm left at Big Mama house was enough to start the investigation on him, but like you said follow my gut. That's just what I'm doing and it tells me that someone in the bureau is assisting this organization." Trent confessed displaying his frustration.

I sat back plotting while Trent was figuring out his place in the bureau. My feelings and concern for others besides the ones that earned it was obsolete by then. Other than those, no fucks were given.

"I don't know why you haven't figured it out yet, Trent. But let me help you out. It's killed or be killed. The type of people like Senior, have enough money, power, and weak souls to buy whatever they may need. If we don't take them out they're going to keep coming for us."

"I know all of that Dylasia. What I can't figure out is how to get rid of them, stay my ass out of prison and keep us alive."

Ding Dong.

The doorbell chimed interrupting us. Trent rose up off the couch with his pistol drawn.

"Answer the door slowly." Trent whispered standing to the side in the foyer.

"Who is it?" I asked sliding the cute metal chute to the side revealing a blonde chick.

I opened the door just enough to see her holding a huge white plastic bag. "Hi, your total is $63.19."

"Okay, here is a $100. Keep the change." I smiled taking the bag and shutting the door closed. I had no time to chit chat. At the time a bitch's stomach was in her back.

Chapter 15

Big Mama, Trent, and I sat at the dining table eating pepper steak, brown rice and mixed vegetables, with garlic knot bread. I was on my fourth glass of Merlot, feeling right. Trent and Big Mama were discussing the upcoming Presidential election. We were all flipping out over Donald Trump running for President. Hell, that racist bastard hadn't even held a political office position in all his lousy days. What was America coming to?

"Hey baby, how are you feeling?" Trent smiled at me then licked his lips causing my thoughts to shift in a totally different direction.

Staring him down my mind was on getting my walls massaged by Trent's thick eight inch wand. Even though, I just told him he was on pussy punishment, I was ready to let him tame my wild side as soon as we got some privacy.

I ran my tongue across my lips slowly and seductively before sipping on my wine. By the time I pulled my mouth back down from the glass, Trent was drooling…

"I'm going to freshen up. Here are the keys to the white Lexus. Big Mama please be careful going to church. There is a GPS system in the car. Just type or say the address and it will navigate directions for you. Here is a prepaid phone. Call us if anything looks out of order and to check in every once in a while. Also, carry this." Trent handed Big Mama a small caliber gun in a pouch along with the other items.

"Oh Lord, they trying to bring the Oakland up out of me, I don't want to do any 187's Trent." Big Mama replied jokingly taking the pouch, phone and car keys.

"Cut it out lady! Just do what he asked please!" I gave her the hint.

"Humph, the same people who are candy to our eyes can be poison to our hearts. Study their ingredients before feeding them to your soul, Dy'. Goodnight Trent." Big Mama said giving me the evil eye as she strolled out of the kitchen and went to go get ready for church.

I couldn't wait until she left the room. My hormones were in a rage and I couldn't wait to tackle Trent.

While he was putting away the food, I walked up behind him. I traced my fingers along his back.

Standing up on my tiptoes and gesturing him down a bit, I placed soft kisses on his neck while my hand massaged his manhood.

"I'm not having sex with you while Big Mama here with us baby." Trent moaned turning around to face me.

"We don't have too." I cooed in his ear as I moved his hand down to my love nest.

Trent scooped me up in his arms so fast I started giggling. I couldn't stop.

Sitting me on the island, I calmed down as our eyes locked then our lips followed. I could feel the passion shooting through my body as the intensity from our kiss deepened.

"Mmm." I moaned as his hands caressed my breast.

"Come on before we get in trouble." He teased blowing on my nipple.

Trent led the way upstairs to a huge loft style master suite. All the way up I was coming out of my clothing, one item at a time. I didn't even make it up the stairs good before I was wearing nothing but my birthday suit. I went straight for the bed.

Lying across the plush California King Mattress set, I spread my legs and toyed with my clit. Trent watched me with an intense stare that turned into one of pure lust as he slowly bit down on his fist.

"I know you not scared of Big Mama are you?" I teased placing my fingers into my mouth making sure they were nice and wet.

Continuing to rub my clit slowly, Trent dropped down to his knees. He then pulled me to the edge of the bed and spread my thighs even wider.

The moment his tongue invaded my sweet spot I creamed all over his lips. "Oowee, please don't stop." I cooed while grinding my hips.

Trent flipped my ass over pulling me into the doggy position. I arched my back making sure he got all access while thinking he was about to treat me to a dick session. Instead of his manhood entering, I felt the wetness of his mouth as it covered my entire vagina. He had me wanting to scream from the top of my lungs but I knew I couldn't. Big Mama would hear me…

"You like that baby?" Trent probed lapping up my juices as he flicked his tongue back and forth on my swollen clit.

"Yes…" I moaned massaging my breast while twisting my hips.

Trent kissed, sucked, and licked me so good I was ready to marry that nigga right then. I had never in my life had a foreplay session like that.

Shit, and then for him not to expect me to return the favor! He was definitely a keeper…

Even though he didn't ask for it, I was in the mood to give him some head. I was turned on just that much.

Twenty minutes later, we laid there exhausted with our minds lost in our own thoughts. While I should have been basking in the ambiance, for some reason flashes of the video I secretly recorded of Ivery and Kelsie raping me invaded my mind. They were unwelcomed and I did everything I could to shake them.

I turned to check to see if Trent was still awake, but he wasn't. I slipped out of bed, grabbed some clothes, quietly got dressed and left out of the room.

It was time for me to cause havoc…

Chapter 16

After I found out that Big Mama had already left for church, I began roaming through the huge six bedroom house. Within minutes, I found what I was looking for.

What I learned about Trent was, he always had a private room where he could handle his job for the bureau. I didn't see why that house would be any different. It wasn't.

Opening the door, I saw two computer monitors to the left of me. A nice cherry oak desk was positioned against the wall. On top of it sat a glass case.

Turning on the reading lamp, I became excited with the toys before me. Trent was ready for war. Amongst the many weapons were cuffs, Tasers with enough volts to put a bear down, along with a variety of guns to choose from.

Taking a little of everything including enough bullets, I hurried up placing everything into a messenger bag with handles that he had sitting next to a chair. I was about to get somewhere and planned to be back before Trent even noticed that I was gone.

Twenty minutes flat due to light traffic, I was back at Senior's house. Reaching into the back seat, I grabbed the bag and removed the night sensor binoculars and checked out the house.

The truck that I saw earlier was still parked and two more vehicles sat in the driveway. I secured the bullet proof vest just the way that Trent did the last time. Next, I stuffed my two small handguns in the lower pocket of my pants and placed the binoculars around my neck.

I felt like a damn fool with all that shit on. Who was I fooling? I didn't know what the hell I was doing but I was going to try to catch somebody slipping.

Tip toeing through a yard nearby, I noticed that everyone was sitting around a table in the dining room chatting. That was when I made my move.

Feeling bold, I crept up the back three stairs and twisted the knob. It was unlocked! I couldn't believe it. "Fuck yes!" Holding my breath I slowly opened the door and entered quietly.

I could hear laughter and people talking so I paused briefly. I stood against the refrigerator and estimated the steps it would to take to get to the next room.

Just as I got ready to move, a Spanish woman, who appeared to be the maid, entered the kitchen. She didn't see me but I couldn't take any chances. Like a lion hunting his prey I stepped lightly. When I got close enough, I tapped her on the shoulder with my gun then covered her mouth.

"Where is Senior?" I quizzed pressing the gun into her back.

She pointed up at the ceiling.

"Take me to him." I spat through clinched teeth.

The maid did as she was asked so we had no problems. That was a good thing.

I moved quietly through the house with her as my shield until she nodded to a room in a corner with the door open some.

Hitting that bitch in the back of her head, she fell down. I left her ass right there and peeked into the room. That dirty ass old man had the nerve to be getting his dick sucked by a pretty young Spanish chick. He must have been paying her real swell.

I stepped back and tried to figure out what I should do. *"There is no backing down now, take him out."* I told myself barging into the room with my eyes trained on Senior.

The Spanish chick looked me up and down then stood back. I smiled slyly and took out my knife swiftly. Next, I snatched Senior's head. Not giving him a chance to speak, I slit his throat from ear to ear. I had no remorse or regret about it.

Blood spewed out everywhere as his corpse slumped over then down onto the grey tiled flooring. I quickly moved out of the trying to avoid the bodily fluid from getting on me.

"Aaaarggh!" The young Spanish girl grunted loudly from the hallway that led to the exit.

I snapped out of it quick, running right by her. I never thought about an escape plan in the midst of my madness.

Making it back to the way I came in, I went out the rear door and approached the stairs. That was when I heard Ivery's voice.

Panic started to get the best of me as I crept back to the doorway and looked in. I kept one foot in and the other outside the house. I wanted some leverage just in case I had to take off running.

Slowly moving my head to the side to gain a better view, the first thing I spotted was a gas hot water heater. I knew that if I could hit it the line then I could blast Ivery's ass out. Yeah, I was reaching but that was the only idea I had at the time.

Searching around in my pocket frantically, I snatched one of the guns out. What I had to do was to aim it right at the metal hoses. I just prayed that I hit the gas line.

Soon as I held my gat up, I saw Ivery's sorry ass across the room. He was standing directly beside the hot water heater.

Our eyes locked instantly, I stuck up my middle finger, and began firing. "Pop, pop, pop."

Boom!

The gas appliance blew up and shook the whole house. Part of it erupted in flames.

That shit knocked me right off the back stoop onto the cold wet grass. I struggled to get up from the blast and limped over to the car fast as I could. I had to get out of there in case anyone saw me or Ivery wasn't dead.

If he wasn't, I knew that the moment he found out his father was dead because of me he would come for me and I'd be waiting. Right then, my only concern was getting back home before Trent realized I wasn't there and then ballistic. He would definitely be worried about me.

Revenge was now being dealt and on my terms. It was only the beginning and I was trying to even the score. Ivery took a piece of my soul by violating me so it was only fair that I took a piece of his lifeline.

Next up on my list, Trent's buddy ol' pal Malcolm...

Chapter 17

The sun was rising when I tried to creep back into the house. That was why I stopped by a twenty-four hour diner to order breakfast. I had to come up with a reason why I was out.

"What you trying to sneak in for? It's all over the news Dy'." Trent snapped turning on the 19' flat screen TV in the kitchen.

Reporting live from KWLV Channel 2 news this is Kimberly Gordon here this morning. We are here in Fountain Hills, Arizona at the home of a well-known organized crime boss by the name of Ivan Senior. Officials say that sometime between four or five this morning someone broke into the home...

The words trailed off in the distance as I stood there in a daze. I didn't even know when Trent left the room. When I turned around, he was just gone.

Rushing into the kitchen then into the living room, I couldn't find Trent anywhere. Suddenly I heard a thumping noise. It was coming from the garage.

"Dylasia!" Trent screamed loud enough for me to hear him from the kitchen.

My stiff body wouldn't move. All the courage I had hours before was gone right out the window. I was scared to face Trent but I knew that I had to.

Slowly traveling towards the sound of his voice, I drug my feet until I reached the door that led to the garage. When I went to twist the knob, Trent came storming out holding the evidence.

"You didn't have sense enough to get rid of this shit? What if they traced this shit back to us? What if someone saw you? What if something would have happened to you?"

Trent dropped everything that he was carrying and grabbed me into a hold. He hugged me tightly for several seconds before he let me go.

"I don't wanna lose you baby." Trent sighed as he picked up the bulletproof vest and weapons.

"I was careful…"

"We'll talk about it when I get back. I have to go clean up your mess right quick."

Trent smacked his lips and hopped in the car that I used to do my dirt. I knew that was the last time seeing that whip.

The garage slowly closed and I let go of the door leading into the house, allowing it to slam noisily. I didn't expect it to be that loud and my first reaction was to jump. I instantly had a flashback of the explosion.

Feeling dirty from the entire event, I went up to the master bedroom and drew me a hot bubble bath. It always made me feel better but I knew it couldn't wash away the horrible memories that played over and over in my head.

While I waited for the tub to fill, I called and checked on Big Mama. "Dy you see the news?"

She answered and started right in. She didn't even give me a chance to say a word until three to four minutes later.

"I'm fine and yes I saw it. I don't know what happened Big Mama," I lied as I crossed my fingers behind my back like I did when I was a little kid.

"That was the same house that they were holding me at!" my grandmother whispered into the phone. "I see that one dude and his dad's picture posted all on the TV but I didn't see the main guy. That was the guy that was in charge."

My mind went in a whirl as I thought of Malcolm being the ringleader. I spent all that time trying to take Senior and Ivery out when I could have easily just started with him. Yeah, he was a slick bastard, but I was about to be slicker…

"Big Mama you just be careful. Whoever it is knows that you got away and that makes you a threat. I would feel much better if you just came back here and stay until they catch that guy." I urged beginning to really worry about the danger my grandmother was in.

Big Mama was stubborn. She was adamant about staying at her all night prayer group meeting. It wouldn't be over until noon and then she had to attend a prayer ceremony after that. The list of hers went on.

"God got me Dy! Don't worry about me, just watch out for that sick man! He has it out for Trent. I don't know why but it has something to do with his wife. Did you know he was married baby?"

"Yes Big Mama, his wife was killed." I tried to explain without going into details.

"Well you need to look into that a little deeper. That guy that was holding me went on and on how he was going to take Trent out and he meant it Dy!" my grandmother informed me.

After assuring her that I would be fine, she hung up with the promise of checking in every couple of hours. I tried to make it once an hour but she wasn't going for it.

I set my cell down and removed all my clothing before stepping my foot down in my relaxing bubble bath. Once I submerged my entire body from the neck down, I took a deep breath and relaxed. The hot steamy water was doing the trick. For the moment…

Chapter 18

After that bath I went to bed and fell asleep within minutes. I was woken up hours later by a hand massaging my thigh. I let out a slight moan before opening up my eyes.

"What the fuck?" I yelled as I started kicking and screaming while trying to fight Ivery off of me. The left side of his face was burnt to a crisp and he was talking shit while choking me out. I swear it felt like I could barely breathe.

"Dy, wake up!" I heard Trent shout.

It was all a dream but that shit seemed so fucking real. I was all choked up and everything.

I hurried and sat straight up in the bed then looked around before Trent held me close. I couldn't stop the tears if I wanted to.

"It seemed so real baby," I cried as I latched on to him even tighter. "It was Ivery! He was alive and he came to kill me!"

Trent let me go and stood up without looking at me. I got the strangest feeling before he began talking.

"Dy, don't panic but there was only one body found in that house. His throat was cut. There was a woman that they found near the scene but she refused to talk. She said that she didn't remember a thing." Trent explained.

"That was Senior! What happened to Ivery? He couldn't have survived that blast Trent! It was way too big and he was pretty damn close!"

"Are you sure he didn't have time to move out of the way?"

I thought hard and tried to remember things just how they happened. That was when I realized that I was so focused on hitting the gas line that I didn't really pay attention to where Ivery was after I start letting rounds off. I put my head down and admitted it to Trent.

"I'm not worried about Ivery too much right now. I need to get to Malcolm." Trent acknowledged as he stripped and joined me in the bed. Yes, it was daylight but we had the thick curtains closed up to create a night time vibe.

"Can we not talk about him right now?" I pleaded as I hovered over him and kissed his cheek then his neck.

Trent wrapped me up in his arms and drew me down to him. "I love you so much baby. I just don't want you to do no stupid shit like that again. What if..."

I placed my finger gently on his lips to shush him. He got silent and closed his eyes before he hugged me again. "It didn't. I'm still here and I'm okay."

Honestly I didn't know how long that was going to hold true. As far as I knew my days were numbered as long as Malcolm and Ivery were alive.

"Ring, ring, beep, beep"

It was Trent's business cell. It was sitting over on the oak dresser with his gold watch and wallet.

"Shit, that might be Malcolm!" he said hopping up out of the bed to go and answer it.

"Oh, fuck it is him!"

"What are you gonna say baby?" I asked anxiously.

Trent held his hand up as he connected the call. "What's up man? Where have you been? I see all this crazy shit on the news about Ivery's house so I rush down to the bureau. When I get down there everyone was asking where the hell you were!"

He was trying to sound worried but all the while he was looking at me shrugging like he didn't know what else to say. The shit was funny but the situation wasn't so I held in my laughter.

"Yeah man, I figured you were with one of ya 'hunnie's'." Trent continued with his charade.

"It's cool I'm just wondering where the hell Ivery went. They said that they identified his father at the house but they didn't say shit about Ivery. You still have someone tailing him?"

Whatever Malcolm was saying, Trent wasn't buying because he was steady shaking his head 'no' while pointing to the phone. He smirked and looked at me as he pushed the mute button on his cell. "This nigga lying!"

He quickly took the mute off and continued talking.

"Aight I guess there aint too much to do right now but wait," Trent sighed.

There was a pause right before Malcolm got a real reaction out of Trent. That shit right there busted that fool right on up.

"Huh, are you talking about Dylasia's grandmother?" Trent asked calmly. "I don't know because I've been with Dy the past twenty four hours and I'm pretty sure she said Big Mama was out of town with the church group. Why would you ask about her?"

Hitting the mute button again Trent squinted at me and twisted his lips up. "This nigga stuttering and shit! What the fuck he asking about Big Mama for? Yeah, because that nigga know he's out of pocket and his ass is cold fucking busted!"

Trent hit 'mute off' and kept right on running his mouth to Malcolm.

"Huh, oh yeah man it's cool. I forgot I told you about her not feeling well. I guess she's better because she sure did get ghost with her church buddies. You know how they get when it's time to praise the Lord." Trent said not knowing what he was talking about. I just shook my head at him.

"Okay meet me in the morning down at the office so we can come up with another plan," Trent suggested. "Unless you hear from the guy that's trailing Ivery. If you do make sure you call me. Right now I'm trying to spend some time with my woman."

Trent checked the time to make sure he kept the call under two minutes. That way Malcolm wouldn't be able to run a trace. Even though it was a secure line, you could detect the area it was coming from if you kept the line live for long enough. Trent wasn't that stupid to slip up.

"What now? You think he bought it?" I questioned the minute Trent disconnected the call and placed his cell back on the dresser.

"I really hope he did. We don't need him going after your grandmother. We might have thrown him off of our trail for the time being but Malcolm is no dummy by far. He calculates shit pretty damn well so we have to be up on our 'P's and Q's' baby."

I picked up the phone to give Big Mama an update of what was going on. She was still adamant about staying at the church. Hopefully Malcolm wouldn't go that far to do no dumb stuff on holy ground. Not up in the Lord's house...

Chapter 19

Trent came back to join me in the bed with a lot of shit on his mind. I could totally understand because I was worried as hell too, just knowing that we didn't have a plan yet. I felt so unprepared.

Looking over at Trent as he snored lightly, I fantasized about what our lives would be like under normal circumstances. I would love that.

Trent did have a lot of qualities that I'd look for in a man. He was intelligent, charming, understanding, outgoing, funny, dick was on point, handsome with an established career in the bureau. Oh yeah, did I mention his dick was on point?

Shit a bitch was winning finally. I could see myself being his wife and fixing him breakfast after an intense love making session before work.

The thoughts brought a smile to my face as I caressed Trent's chest then wrapped up in his arms. As we lay there, our heartbeats became in sync. The soothing rhythm helped me drift off to sleep.

Beep... Beep... An annoying sound echoed throughout the house. I couldn't see how the hell Trent was sleeping through the shit.

I jarred up, alert as ever then pulled the cover back swinging my legs over the edge of the bed. The noise continued and seemed to be getting louder than before. *Beep... Beep... Beep...*

"What the hell!" I huffed making my way all the way out the bed. Trent was still out like a light sleeping peacefully.

I followed the irritating beeping noise all the way to Trent's office. I opened the door and fiddled around for the round dimming switch. Turning the knob to bring the lights up enough so I could see inside, I began feeling my way around until I got closer to the machine that was still sounding off. It was the fax near his desk.

I quickly pressed the button with the green flashing light to shut the noise up. I was tired as hell and restless.

Not wanting to pry, something nagged at me to take a peek at the fax Trent received. There were over a dozen documents.

"Go to bed Dylasia," I had to tell myself as I turned to leave.

Beep... Beep... Beep... The machine started up again. I stood there reading the word 'classified' on every page. I wanted to know what why they were marked that way so I retrieved the papers, shut the light back off, and headed in the room with Trent.

Whatever they were I was sure that he would want to see them too. I just had to scan through them first.

Nestled up nice and cozy next to him, I read what appeared to be a case file. I flipped the papers over.

"Oh shit!" I gasped startling Trent a little. He began stirring a bit so I sat real still for a moment until he settled into another snore.

When he was calm again, I started to read the documents beginning with the cover sheet. It was an email from an 'Agent Carlisle' informing Trent of the contents of the file. I nodded my head side to side, I felt like I was on my own episode of Law & Order, and I was Detective Benson reading over the police reports.

"What the hell?" I gasped as kept reading the witnesses statements of the men and women rescued from the human trafficking raids.

The pictures weren't capturing my attention until I picked up one of Malcolm and Trent's wife holding hands in front of a car with valet. There were also several shots of them kissing and hugging. Attached to the pics was a brief summary.

August 06, 2014 7:09 p.m Special Agent Lorraine Gresham & Malcolm Holmes -- Surveillance #B3224 Agent Malcolm having dinner with Sonoita Cartel El Jeffe Senior. Ocean's Prime Steakhouse.

My mind was blown by the relationship between Malcolm and Lorraine, Trent's deceased wife. They were saying a lot more than the two being in a relationship, so much more. I read all about the secret love affair. No one was loyal these days...

I sat that set of info to the side and concentrated on the ones that talked about Lorraine's sister Lorreal. She was still alive and had been seen with Ivery and Sydney on many occasions. Every little detail was documented. Some details were marked over with a permanent marker or something. I ignored them and tried to wake Trent up. I wondered if he could make sense of all the evidence. It still seemed like there was a missing link.

"Trent! Baby get up!" I shook him frantically. By now I had pictures scattered across the floor of the bedroom. I had Malcolm's personal files laid out right along with Ivery's.

"What's wrong baby? Lay back down." Trent mumbled half sleep pulling the covers up over his head.

"Trent get the hell up now! We have work to do!" I demanded standing next to the bed, hands on my hips.

"Fuck!" Trent huffed sitting up looking around at my arrangement of papers.

"I'll make us a pot of coffee." I said picking up the main document. Trent was still upright on the bed looking confused.

"Oh, while you were sleeping the fax machine continuously went off. This is what was sent to you." I informed him handing him the cover letter of the fax before disappearing off to go to the kitchen.

I knew in my heart that the betrayal of his felonious wife was going to have Trent irate. After all he did believe he was building a family with that bitch.

Now the tables had turned and instead of wondering, not really knowing what happened, Trent would finally have the answers he was looking for. Even though I knew he wouldn't like it, I think that he needed it.

I felt sorry for all parties involved. I was so ready to end the fuckery. All I wanted was a little peace. That was all I wanted…

Chapter 20

When I came back into the room, Trent and I sat down on the extra thick chocolate brown carpeting of his bedroom floor. We were analyzing all the key points of the investigation. I could sense he was uptight about the facts he now knew about his wife and Malcolm. The one issue that nagged us was trying to determine if Agent Lorraine was working with Malcolm all along or did she find herself tangled in a dangerous web. I asked Trent to see how he felt about it and what our next move would be.

"So what do we do about the sister now that we know she's alive?" I questioned him.

"We get her to a safe spot, I'll record her statement while we interview her. That's another major break in my case. I just can't believe all this time Malcolm was in on the whole thing and I didn't suspect anything. He had Lorraine to thank for that!" Trent spat.

"Look at me!" I demanded taking my hand to his chin to turn him to face me. "What you're not going to do is blame or feel sorry for yourself. Obviously Lorraine was eating her cake and ice cream too. I know it hurts being deceived but the damage is done and there isn't anything that you can do to change it. Anyway, a chick trifling enough to play with a child is not the woman to bear your child. You were too good for her anyway. I know that now since I've read her file!" I expressed to Trent leaning in placing a soft kiss on his lips.

He smiled. "Thanks baby, it's not that though. Something else is bothering me." Trent admitted reading the rest of Malcolm and Lorraine file.

I rubbed his shoulder as he pulled up images of receipts records, phone messages, and the pictures of his wife and Malcolm together on numerous occasions.

"Got you motherfucker!" Trent shouted cross referencing the messages with pictures.

"What?" I quizzed being nosey.

"Malcolm texted Lorraine right around the same time she was killed according to the Coroners report of time of death. Then she received instructions from a number linked to one of the Sonoita Cartel members..." Trent paused for a second shuffling papers around frantically.

"This is the link!" He yelled holding up the police report and mugshot booking picture up of a young Ivery.

"Wait! Let me see if I follow you. So Malcolm, back when he worked as a DEA agent, locked Ivery up on a major bust. Senior, his father, got to Malcolm some type of way which resulted in Ivery's charges disappearing, and now with Malcolm working for the bureau and the cartel it made them untouchable. Lorraine was a pawn until you came along almost ruining Malcolm's perfect plan. Lorraine and Malcolm were secretly sleeping together before she even became involved with you but didn't know how to tell you she was in too deep with Malcolm. She had to know Trent... Oh my God! Malcolm killed your wife!" I paced back and forth twirling my hair making sense of what was utter chaos.

This shit was better than the shows I watched on Lifetime; it was live in color.

Trent got up, obviously processing the turn of events. I stood over the desk and looked at the address of where Lorreal was. It stuck out at me like a sale at Nordstroms.

"Trent we gotta go! We need to get to the sister, leave a trail so Malcolm comes to us, and we'll be waiting. The cards are in our favor, we got the juice now thanks to Agent Carlisle." I said getting hyped up. My man quickly switched it up and put the moves on me.

"No, not right now though. Planning, remember?" he whispered.

Trent cupped my chin observing me very closely. The way his eyes pierced my soul made my heart beat faster. Then to increase the pace even more, I allowed his lips to invade mine. Our tongues were speaking the words we wanted to say. Our bodies followed and before I knew it we were making sweet love, over and over again, taking short breaks in between to catch our breath.

"Mmmm." I cooed when he brought me up for air for the last time then took my high down when he started discussing business. I didn't even want to think about that shit.

It had been a whole three hours and it hadn't crossed my mind one time. That was the longest I had peace in months…

"I think we got the juice. But before we make any moves I want to spend some time enjoying you. Once we get Big Mama situated we'll take care of Malcolm and Ivery. Right now you are my only concern."

I couldn't disagree and complain like I wanted to. I couldn't poke my lip up and start pouting. So, instead I stood there and watched him organize the paperwork.

When I looked around I noticed the mess we had made. "Damn, I need to get this shit up."

Bending down, I cleaned up the plates of fruit and cheese we snacked on and our coffee cups. I took everything to the kitchen and headed back to the bedroom. When I stepped inside, it was empty. Right away I went searching for Trent and soon found him in his office. He was standing there on a video call with Agent Carlisle clarifying everything that he faxed over to him.

I didn't want to interrupt, so I remained quiet and squeezed his butt cheek playfully then excused myself. I was going to go freshen up and see what Trent and I could get into in order to put an end to the bullshit.

Chapter 21

It was early afternoon when Big Mama finally made it in from prayer group. She was feeling very talkative. She was going on and on about how the Bishop Turner laid hands over her and the prayer warriors prayed with the holy oil to let her lust go. Big Mama had us cracking up.

"I'm telling y'all the Lord knows our issues even before we do. And lately my issue is I need some loving… I don't want to die alone. Heck, I aint been with a man since your granddaddy died. I need someone to knock the dust out child! That's why I got me a date with the fine Minister Percy Howard tomorrow night." Big Mama confessed.

"I'm happy for you Big Mama! Now let me run a background and financial report before you step out on your date." Trent joked.

"Boy, don't play Trent! I need to know all that information now since you brought it up." Big Mama replied standing there holding her favorite purple bible. "You never can be too careful can you? Aint that what they say?"

"Yes and we had to learn that the hard way too Big Mama." I smiled.

"Unfortunately yes, but that's a good thing too." She replied.

"Why's that Big Mama?" Trent asked.

"Because now we can say as you young folk say, 'stay two steps ahead'." She giggled like it was the funniest thing on earth. "Now I'm gonna leave, take my bible right here, go to my borrowed room, say my prayers and go ahead on and get some sleep. You two need me, you know where I'll be."

My grandmother went to bed while Trent and I tried to spend a little quality time together. Ever since all the life threatening drama began, we hadn't had the chance to enjoy each other's company like we used to outside of sex. I was curious how it would be since our chemistry was now on a new level.

We started out watching movies then played a few games of pool. Of course I spanked his tail.

Next, we enjoyed the smooth sweet taste of mixed fruit margaritas I made for us. I was on my third round when we started playing a game of dominoes.

"Watch me do this right here Dy! Run me my bones shawty!" Trent bragged teasing me as he placed his domino down locking the board. I slowly turned over my bones one by one and added up what I got caught with in my hand.

"Oh hell yeah, what's that right there?" Trent clowned bending forward on the table while putting his hand up to his ear like he was trying to hear me better. "What, what ya say that there is right there huh?"

I laughed at his lingo and repeated my total. "I said sixty three for sixty five!"

Trent teased me as he moved his peg up on the cribbage board we were using to keep score. Every move forward counted as five points. The first one around the board won.

"Oh yeah, what are we playing for tonight baby?" Trent flirted by licking his lips while looking downward.

"You don't know?"

"What?"

"You don't have to win to get that."

"What about a little special treatment to go with it?" Trent pushed.

"That goes both ways?"

"Yep, anything goes…" Trent said while waiting for me to confirm.

"Anything baby!"

Trent shoved all the dominoes my way and I began mixing them around. He hurried up and snatched his up and slapped down the big five. "Ten my friend!"

"Ugh!"

Two plays later he was yelling fifteen and the next one after that he was hollering again. "Twenty twin twin… Nigga!" After that, it was all she wrote! Trent spanked my ass by making it around the board in five short rounds.

"Okay, now on to that special treatment that we discussed."

"We're gonna have to take that up to the bedroom baby," I suggested as I led the way.

"Damn! Here we go again!" I shouted as the fax alert began sounding off. "What the hell do you have that shit set on?"

The loud noise was about to drive me crazy. I waited for Trent to shut off the machine before I went in his study after him to be nosy.

"It only does it when it's from Agent Carlisle." Trent explained as he began pulling the documents from the tray one by one. "I had it set like that because he only faxes me things from that number when it's an emergency."

If I had antennae's they would have stood right up. "So this is another emergency?"

"Yeah, Agent Carlisle wants me to move in on Lorraine's sister right now. She is apparently alone and now is a good time to go." Trent stated as he snatched up all the papers and headed to the bedroom.

As we both began to get dressed, Trent stopped and looked at me. "Where are you going?"

"With you, where you think?" I responded while still getting my clothes on.

"No, no, you need to stay here with Big Mama!" Trent insisted with no luck. "Don't you want to make sure your grandmother is safe?"

"Shit, Big Mama can hold her own. Don't you know that by now?" I fussed as I slipped my Adidas on and tied them up.

"You are so fucking hardheaded, I swear Dy!" Trent gritted his teeth and grabbed his cell and the paperwork.

I dug in my handbag removing my ID case then slid it into my back pocket, afterwards making sure to slide my phone in my front one. By the time I got to the top of the stairs, I heard the garage door open.

"Wait Trent!" I yelled out forgetting all about Big Mama sleeping.

I covered my mouth and flew out to the garage only to see Trent standing there dangling the keys. "If you're gonna go, you're gonna drive. I need to go over a few things in these documents anyway."

Trent tossed me the keys and we were off. I was so damn glad he didn't try to fight me about it…

Chapter 22

A couple of hours later we arrived in Sierra Vista. It was just a little southeast of Tucson Arizona and only a few short miles to the Mexican Border. It was an easy way for any of them to flee.

"Do you think we should've told Big Mama we were leaving?" I asked Trent as I made our last turn leading to the house where Lorreal was supposedly at. "Call Agent Carlisle and make sure his satellite images are still showing it's safe to go in."

When Trent didn't answer, I turned to him only to see that he was already using the phone. He said a few words and hung up.

"What did he say?"

"He said because of the high winds the video went blank for a few minutes a couple of times." He sighed sounding really irritated.

"So what you want to do?" I asked as I pulled up and parked a little ways away from the house. We could still see it in the distance, but it was far enough to stay discreet.

"Let's creep up there and see what we can find out. If something doesn't look right then we can call for backup."

"Why didn't they have backup out here already?"

"Because we don't know who we can trust right now. If we take a chance and give the info to the wrong person the whole case could be blown. We sure in the hell don't want that shit to happen." Trent fussed as we got out of the car as quietly as we could.

We agreed to stay together since we didn't have anyone to watch the perimeter except for the satellite and that shit couldn't come save us! "There's a light on in the side room."

We walked around the outside of the whole house and property. It looked more like a fucking plantation to me by the way the place was built. The huge cactuses that were oddly shaped surrounding the area gave you that Wild Wild West feel.

"Look," Trent pointed at the vehicles that were parked back off in the cut. "Why are they hiding their cars?"

"I don't know?" I smirked. "Why the hell are we sneaking in when you can just go and knock on the door and ask to speak with her?"

"Because I don't know who the hell could be with Lorraine and honestly I don't know if I can trust her." Trent answered truthfully.

"Enough said!"

We kept going until we made a complete circle around the house. Noticing that the whole house was dark with the exception of a closet light that was on in one of the bedrooms that was located on the west side of the place. "There has to be more than one person in there."

"We don't know that. Let's just go inside so we can see. You want to talk to Lorreal don't you? She might have all the answers we need to put Ivery and Malcolm away for good!"

"Yeah, you're right Dy."

"Come on then," I whispered heading to the back until Trent stopped me in my tracks.

"Let's go in the front door. I can see no one is in there." Trent suggested as he held on to my hand and led the way up the four small stairs and onto the wrap-around porch.

Trent went to the door and twisted the knob expecting it to be open. "It's locked."

"You think?" I whispered looking at the old wooden door.

Reaching into my back pocket, I drew out my case and pulled my ID out. I turned it sideways and slid it into the slit on top of where the lock was. As I jiggled the handle lightly so I wouldn't make any noise, I moved my plastic drivers' license up and down until it opened.

Trent looked at me and turned his lips up as I put my ID back in my pants and crept in behind him. When we entered, I gently closed the door before a draft came through and alerted Lorreal that we were there.

When we got fully inside, we could hear some soft music playing. It was coming from the back. We slowly walked through the living room being careful not to trip over anything. It was pretty dark. The only light was coming from the moon shining through the window. The ray rested right upon the far right wall.

I nudged Trent as I looked at all the pictures of Lorreal. She was dressed up so fancy in all the photos.

There was one in particular that caught my eye though. It was both Trent's wife Lorraine and her sister. I watched as he got closer to take another look.

"Ah, oh!" I heard over the music. I guess Trent heard it too because he stepped to me and covered my mouth with his hand. I wasn't even talking.

I jerked his hand away and gave him that look. I knew the drill.

"Oooo shit! Yes nigga!" a voice yelled out. I didn't know who it was.

"Bend yo ass over!" I heard Malcolm demand. I knew it was him! I knew that voice for sure.

"Damn, he in there fucking Lorreal?" I whispered with a frown of disgust. "After he done fucked her sister too? That's some dirty shit!"

Trent shushed me and eased nearer to the open room. The noises were getting louder.

"Lo, you bout to make me bust right in you!" Malcolm warned. He obviously wasn't using a damn condom.

I shook my head stared at Trent who had just stopped dead in his tracks. I nearly bumped into the back of him. Before I could speak a word, he was holding his hand up as to tell me to shut the hell up.

Quietly getting on my tiptoes, I peeked over Trent's shoulder to see what he was looking at.

"You know yo shit is so tight!"

"Fuck me! Just shut the hell up and fuck me harder!" Lorreal yelled out.

I watched how Malcolm plunged in and out of her from behind. He had a handful of her hair and was jerking her head back and forth with every pump.

"Malcolm shit!" Lorraine screamed out with her titties bouncing all over the place. She grabbed them both and held on to them as she got fucked violently from behind.

"Bitch be still!" Malcolm ordered as he stood all the way upright and made the ugliest fuck face ever. That nigga looked like he was about to shit on himself but instead he pulled out and busted out on Lorreal's big ass. I knew she had to have implants because her behind was on swole.

While I was into the sex show, I felt Trent moving around. When I looked to see what he was doing, I saw that he had his nine out. I was right with him.

"You are one nasty grimy ass son of a bitch!" Trent yelled catching both Malcolm and Lorraine off guard. "You fuck my wife and now you're fucking her sister? Both of y'all are foul as hell!"

Malcolm jumped so fast and tried to go for his gun as Lorreal ran for cover. When she did, all I could see was a big ass dick swinging. My mouth fell wide the fuck open.

"Pop, pop"

Trent fired two shots at Malcolm to stop him from going to his weapon. It scared the shit out of me for just a second. Then my focus was right back on Lorreal.

"Did you see that Trent!" I yelled pointing to the closet door where Lorreal was hiding.

"Naw, what you tripping on Dy?" he questioned as Lorreal ran to the door to escape.

Trent and I were both stunned that neither one of us took a shot. We both just stood there until we noticed Malcolm moving.

Trent turned in just enough time to let off a round and pierce Malcolm in his right hand. It caused him to drop his government issued weapon before he could get off a shot.

"Go get her, he, she, it… Whatever the fuck Dy! Just go get Lorraine.

By the time I made it to the front door there were sirens in the distance along with a helicopter flying above us. The Feds were coming…

Chapter 23

Not wanting to give up my search for Lorreal, I ran down the back road of the property and passed by Trent's car. Soon as I got down a ways, I heard his cell ringing. I rushed back and got it out to answer it.

"Hello?" I panted.

"Who is this?" a man asked. It was Trent's business cell so I knew it had to be Agent Carlisle.

"This is Dylasia and Trent is in the house with Malcolm. He had the gun on him when I ran out but…"

All of a sudden there were two gunshots. I panicked and ran towards the house forgetting all about Agent Carlisle on the phone.

When I got to the front stairs I heard him yelling. "What is going on?"

"I heard shots! Come and help!" I yelled almost falling to the ground before entering back into the house.

"You won't get away with this!" Trent grunted as if he was in pain.

I went and got in the same spot that we were snooping from before. I could see Trent on the ground holding on to his arm. Malcolm had his gun aimed at him as he was walking closer.

Sweat dripped down from my forehead as I pulled my gun out and took a deep breath. "Please let this first bullet hit his ass. I may not have to get a second one off."

I prayed silently as I stepped out into the open and fired three rounds in Malcolm's direction. Not one hit his ass because that nigga was bobbing and weaving.

Out the corner of my eye, I could see Trent trying to get somewhere. He rolled under the table and went for the gun that was on the floor across the room.

Malcolm must have seen him too because he put his aim right back on Trent. He was a little too slow though because the tactical team busted right in and tackled his ass. Butt naked and all…

"Are you two okay?" a young officer asked. "You must be the infamous Agent Trenton Santiago. I'm Agent Dale. I was sent by Agent Carlisle."

"Password," Trent smirked like he wasn't about to say shit.

Agent Dale bent down and whispered something into Trent's ear. When the guy stood back up, the two shook hands.

"Where did the woman go?" he questioned referring to Lorreal.

"The woman?" Trent commented sarcastically. "Well, she had both tits and a dick so I really don't know what the hell it is?"

Agent Dale's face turned as red as Rudolph's nose when it shined so bright. He didn't know what to say and when he did try to speak he began stuttering. I didn't blame him because I was in shock too. I had never seen no shit like that in my life. And to think Malcolm was fucking him in the ass! Old shitty motherfucker...

The whole operation was sick as hell and was so way out there that I was having a hard time at grasping reality. Everything that I was seeing and experiencing was some twisted shit you would see in a movie or read in one of those Urban Fiction Novels.

"Okay, okay, okay then..." Agent Dale blurted out. "So he or I mean she got away?"

"Well I didn't think she was a suspect." Trent admitted as he placed his arm around me.

"You must have not gotten Agent Carlisle's last fax."

"Ah, no I've been gone from the house for a couple of hours."

"Don't you have a fax in your government issues sedan?" he asked.

"Yes I do but I'm not driving that car right now. That would have been too noticeable."

Trent shook his head, smirked and began to walk away, dragging me with him. I wanted to ask the agent a few questions but I went right on along with my man because I knew he was upset.

When we stepped outside, they were putting Malcolm in the back of a black Tahoe. Trent stopped and went over to where he was. The officers that were holding on to him let go and backed off.

"I hope all this foul shit you've done was worth whatever you were getting out of it because it's over. It's over for you Malcolm. You have hurt and destroyed too many lives. Your days are numbered you sick sack of shit!"

Malcolm laughed and taunted Trent enough for him to punch him dead in his grill. Malcolm wiped the blood from his mouth and began talking mad shit.

"Nigga this is much bigger than you know. Yeah, you caught me, but I'm not the big fish. Y'all can't even touch him or stop his operation. His money is long and he is international."

We all stood there in shock as we listened to him damn near snitch on his boss. He had to have gone on running his mouth for at least three or four minutes before the stupid fool realized that what he was saying could be used against him in a court of law.

"Aint that some shit, and he works for the damn law!"

As they shoved Malcolm into the rear of the truck head first, Trent stepped back and watched. He didn't stop staring until they drove off. That was when he looked down at me.

"Let's go baby. We got work to do..."

Chapter 24

When we got back to Trent's house out in Buckeye hours later, he went straight to his office to check out the faxes that Agent Dale were referring to. The ones that he said Agent Carlisle sent over.

While he did that, I took my things upstairs then came back downstairs. Traveling into the kitchen, I went and poured me a stiff shot of Jack Daniel's Rose. I drank it down in two gulps and poured another one.

"That bitch had a damn dick!" I laughed as I walked into the den, sat on the sofa and kicked my feet up for a second. I still couldn't believe that shit.

Right as I got comfortable. I heard my cell ringing from upstairs. At first I wasn't about to climb that long ass staircase to get it, but after three calls I got irritated hearing Rihanna's joint *'Work'* as my caller tone. "That shit really 'work, work, work, my nerves!'" I sang to the rhythm of the song.

After sitting there for a few more seconds, I sighed heavily as I peeled myself up from the couch and walked to the foyer. I looked up then began taking the stairs two at a time.

"Who the hell can that be?" I didn't have any friends, Big Mama was asleep, and curiosity was getting the best of me.

Instead of walking around the bed, I hopped across it and grabbed my phone off Trent's nightstand. It was still ringing.

The number was unfamiliar but I answered it anyway sounding highly annoyed that the person had already called what seemed like over a dozen times. The shit better had been important.

"Hello?" I answered with an attitude. No one answered. Instead, there was silence with ragged breathing.

"I know a motherfucker didn't blow my line up to breathe!" I spat ending the call.

Once I hit end, I scrolled through my missed calls and noticed that all of them had been from the number that had just hit me up and didn't say shit.

Ignoring it totally, I tucked my phone in my back pocket and went back downstairs to the den to get cozy on the couch. On my way I stopped by the kitchen to grab another drink. That was when the ringing began all over again.

I was so annoyed that I snatched it out of my pocket. The first thing I did was check to see who it was.

"What the fuck?" I spat when I saw the call was from the same damn number.

"No time to have you lurkin', him act like he don't like it, you know I dealt with you the nicest..."

"Don't keep playing on my fucking phone! Your ass should be dead! You should be nasty old maggot food six feet under by now!" I shouted not prepared to hear his voice.

He paid no attention to what I was saying. Obviously he didn't call me for all that. He just wanted me to listen to the bullshit he had to say.

"I see ya' little captain save-a-hoe came to ya' rescue again. I thought we were better than this Dylasia. I still can smell the fresh scent of that pretty pussy of yours. Come to daddy." Ivery teased belittling me.

"Listen to yourself, sounding just like a fuck boy! It's really pathetic! As handsome as you are you have to take pussy? Nah, don't answer that shit. I already know why! It's cause you a dick-in-the booty ass nigga just like Malcolm and the rest of your damn crew! I should have put a hot slug in your ass when I had the chance. Don't call my fucking phone no more unless you ready to see me bitch ass I-v-e-r-y." I read his ass better than a sign artist signing for the death then hung up in his face.

That clown ass closet dick eater, really came for me. "Damn, why didn't I just act like I wanted to see him? I probably could've played his ass into seeing me.

I dialed the number back and it went straight to the voicemail which was of course full. I gave it several more tries before I came to the conclusion that he either blocked my number or powered his cell off.

Feeling defeated, I sat my phone down and enjoyed the shot that I had just poured myself. That made it three...

At the time that seemed like the perfect solution to calm my nerves. I knew once it hit me I would be relaxed. That was up until I told Trent about the call. Now that was going to be whole different argument.

"Might as well make it four!" I laughed as I continued pouring. Just as I was about to take it to the head, my phone rang.

Staring at my screen lighting up, I saw that it was Ivery. I used that chance to put my plan in motion. I would just have to fill Trent in on it later.

I answered my cell, this time baiting his stupid ass. "What the fuck do you want Ivery?"

His sadistic laughter sent chills over me and the more he played with me, the angrier a bitch was getting. It was like he was rubbing it in my face that he raped me. Then, he had the nerve to act like he would do it again if he had the chance.

It was taking everything in me not to flip my fucking script on that nothing ass nigga! Yeah, that was just what the hell he was. Ugh, I never hated anyone in my life until Ivery entered in to it. He was a wolf in sheep's clothing.

"You think you're tough because of your fake ass superhero, but you're not. I can reach out and touch you right now if I wanted too. That's not my purpose for this call, I want to kiss and make up." Ivery replied sinisterly like he was fooling me. "If you do this one thing for me I promise to never bother you or your sorry ass boyfriend again."

Damn, Ivery was making it so easy for me to set him up. It had to be a catch to it. I wasn't that damn naïve, but I sure made it seem like I was. By then I was positive that Ivery thought that I was still that weak ass bitch he met at the strip club. Oh no buddy, I was so much more than that. He was about to see.

"Meet me at midnight in Piestewa Park over in East Phoenix by the start of the Dreamy Draw Nature Trail. Don't be late either!" I instructed then hung up.

"Ol' fake ass nigga!" I huffed as Trent entered the den where I was sitting. I hung up and stared at him praying he didn't overhear my conversation.

"Baby, this case is getting shittier by the minute. Guess what the fax contained in my office?" Trent quizzed sitting beside me then answered his own question. "That Lorreal, it/him, whatever the hell it is, is the leader of the Sonoita Cartel. Lorreal was Senior's trick up his sleeve. Not only that, he ordered Malcolm to kill Lorraine his own sister. I guess dancing with the devil doesn't work in ya' favor." Trent explained.

"What?" I shouted.

"Wait, thing is that no one knows that Lorreal is really a man except Ivery, Sidney and

Malcolm. Everyone else thinks 'it' is just a tough ass woman!" Trent explained. "Shit, had my ass fooled too. I hadn't a fucking clue!"

"So Lorreal is fooling everybody in the Sonoita Cartel?" I questioned as my head started to pound listening to Trent. "Just think of what they are gonna do to her, I mean him, when they find out!"

"Let's stop calling 'it' Lorreal. His government name is Lorenzo Graham. He's the youngest of three children, with Lorraine being the oldest. I'm going in to the bureau to witness Malcolm hand over his boss Lorreal." Trent informed before kissing me on the cheek. "I have to make sure this fool does the right thing."

"Do you think he'll really give up Lorreal, I mean Lorenzo?" I questioned. "If he did that it would expose Lorreal's true identity. Then The Cartel will come after every last one of them that knew about him being a man, including Malcolm! Jail couldn't even keep his ass safe!"

"Yeah, but let's hope that Malcolm is too damn dumb to figure that one out." Trent sighed and gave me a kiss. "Let me get up out of here. Call me if you need me."

"That's fine, I'm exhausted just wake me up when you get in."

"I will definitely wake you up." Trent cooed in my ear. "Oh yeah, and don't take yo ass out of the house Dy!"

"What if I need some fresh air?"

"Open a damn window!" Trent clowned.

I kissed his lips and waited for him to walk away first. When he did, I disappeared upstairs to prepare for my meeting with Ivery.

All the while I was gathering my necessities for my hit, I thought about telling Trent what I had set up.

"The last time I rode solo, I almost got myself killed!" I thought remembering back to what happened out at Senior's house. With that flashback, I got scared for a minute.

Within seconds, that fear turned into a burning sensation of revenge and I had to listen to it. That was the only way I could keep focused on the matter at hand.

"I gotta take this nigga out! He doesn't deserve to live." I ranted silently. "God, I know that only you can judge, but I have to make this right. So, if I'm wrong please forgive me."

As I thought about what I had planned for Ivery, a sneaky grin crept on my face. Taking him out for every life he ruined was the pleasure I was about to receive.

Within hours, Ivery's stank ass would be in for a rude awakening...

Chapter 25

It was a quarter after seven that evening when Big Mama emerged out of the room ready for her date with Minister Percy Howard. She was wearing a two-piece pastel pink skirt set. Her shoulder length hair in soft curls flowing around her chubby sun kissed brown complexioned face.

I admired my grandmother's attire by winking at her. She immediately began to twirl around so that I could get a better look at her outfit.

"Where are you going Big Mama dressed in your first Sunday clothes?" I teased and brushed her shoulder.

"I'm going to see a man about riding his horse." Big Mama cracked up with her eyebrows raised as she eyed me closely.

"Oh wow, you are too much for TV! Seriously, where are you going?" I grilled her not letting up.

"If you must know child, I'm going to dinner at the Desert Diamond Casino in Glendale." Big Mama finally told me staring in her compact mirror as she applied a light coat of bronzer to her skin.

"Now was that so hard?" I asked straightening out her black silk sheer blouse for her. Even though my Big Mama was sixty-four years young, she still had as much finesse as someone my age.

"Did Trent do that check for me?" Big Mama questioned.

I turned to the table where the credit report and background check was lying. I picked it up, scanned over the two documents then handed it to her.

"I know you seen this. Minister Percy has a computer software company he sold a few years back. Oh, and he owns several properties in the metro area of Phoenix." She bragged ultimately pleased with Trent's findings.

"Yeah, I saw that Big Mama!" I laughed. "Did you already know?"

Before she got the chance to answer me, someone was at the door. It had to be my grandmother's date. Oh lawd...

Ding Dong... The doorbell chimed focusing our attention to the diamond willow hand carved double doors. They each had oval beveled glass windows with etchings. That made the outside image blurry so I couldn't positively identify who it was.

"It must be your friend." I teased with a smile but all the while being protective.

Removing the small .25 caliber from out of the waist of my jeans, I ushered her to the door. Standing to the side, I stood there waiting for Big Mama to open the door.

When she did, we both stared at Minister Percy standing there on the front stoop grinning from ear to ear. Big Mama smiled and turned to me before leaving.

"Yes ma'am and don't wait up for me. We're staying at the resort. Love you Dylasia..." my grandmother said while taking her date's hand.

"Good evening gorgeous." Minister Percy greeted Big Mama smiling.

That man was clean as an old school Cadillac. He had on his black brim hat, pink tie, handkerchief, black blazer and slacks. I knew that his crocodile loafer shoes screamed a few zeros. I glanced at my grandnother who was blushing gazing into Percy eyes.

"Hey, how are you Minister Percy? I'm Dylasia, nice to meet you."

"Hi Miss Dylasia. Nice meeting you as well. I'll return your grandmother soon." He promised.

"I hope so!" I thought silently as I continued to smile.

"Are you ready my leading lady?" Percy flirted with Big Mama while intertwining his arm through hers.

"I sure am. See you later Dy' and tell my grandson I said thank you." Big Mama said winking at me as they left out.

I was excited to see my grandmother happy and still able to enjoy herself. Meanwhile it was time to have a little fun of my own....

****

Trent was home and knocked out by ten thirty and Big Mama was staying out all night. That made it simple to sneak out and make it to the park a little early.

When I got to the garage to hop in the car that Big Mama had been using, I noticed that Trent's vehicle wasn't in there. It was odd because he never parked his car outside.

I opened the garage door and pulled out only to see it parked near the front door. It wasn't even in the driveway.

"What he do that for though?" I thought to myself as I used the control to close the garage.

As I crept by the front of Trent's house, I noticed the light on in the Foyer. "Wasn't that off?"

I seriously couldn't remember but it still seemed weird.

"Maybe I'm tripping," I sighed not having time to worry about it. "I'm gone now so no one can stop me.

I drove off feeling confident about what I was going to do to Ivery as soon as he came in sight. I wasn't going to taunt him or bring up his past crimes. Just 'pop-pop' and he was going to be no longer breathing. I didn't have time for the bullshit. He knew what he had done and so far had shown no remorse for the shit. It was his time to go and I was about to send his ass there special delivery.

I boosted myself up all the way to the park. It took me a whole forty-five minutes to get there.

"Damn!"

I smirked when I went to park in the lot and saw that it was closed at that hour. Since that was the closest way to get to the meeting spot, I had to resort to using my GPS to I find another place to park the car.

Quickly, I located a location off in the cut to hide my car because parking was prohibited on residential streets. I didn't give a damn because I only planned on being there a few minutes.

Once I got out and changed my portable GPS to 'walk' mode, I discovered that I only had to travel a few minutes to get to the trail from where I was. I checked the time and saw that I had ten minutes before Ivery got there.

Hurrying to pick up the pace, I watched my surroundings carefully as I tiptoed as quietly as possible. The air was silent except for the sounds of crickets. That was good though because that meant no witnesses. If I murked him then I would be in the clear.

I surveyed the area once more before I crouched down behind the 'Dreamy Draw' sign next to a canvas of rocks. Once I got my weapon out, I stayed still and waited...

Chapter 26

I felt real comfortable about the spot I chose to hide at because the sign and rocks prevented anyone from seeing me. Plus, I had the perfect view.

"What the hell was that?" I whispered as I jumped up after feeling something slither across my foot. It was a fucking snake!

I must have hopped up like my ass was on fire. I hurried over across the way to find another large tree to hide behind. After seeing that snake I was spooked. Shit, I knew that there had to be more.

Even though I had on my calf high very durable hiking boots, I was still leery. That was one of the things I hated about Arizona. They had Gila Monsters, snakes, scorpions, black widows, brown recluses and many more things that could harm and maybe even kill you. I had to be real careful.

What I had to do was clear my mind and focus. My body was well protected and I kept reminding myself so I wouldn't get freaked out by the reptiles and insects.

Recalling that I had my phone, I checked it and saw that I was already slipping. It was still powered on. I immediately shut it all the way off and tucked it away. I didn't need any interruptions.

Overhearing leaves shuffling nearby, I posted up ready to pounce on my prey. My palms became clammy, my adrenaline was pumping. I was ready to show that clown Ivery a thing or two...

"I don't wanna kill you Dylasia!" I heard a familiar voice whisper as I was grabbed in a headlock from behind. "But, if I don't then Ivery will kill me. He's already killed everyone else I ever loved."

Sidney seemed as if he had lost everything and didn't have anything to live for. That along with the gun he was holding up to my head was enough to know he was dangerous.

"That's what the fuck I get for not bringing Trent," I fussed silently in my head while getting ready to meet my maker.

"What do you want?"

"I want this to be over and the only way I can end it and have peace is by killing you." Sidney replied with a shaky voice but a steady hand.

"Well then I guess you gotta go nigga!" I heard Trent grunt as he knocked Sidney out cold.

"Why didn't you just shoot him?" I snapped before Trent hushed me.

"Because I don't know who else is out here and the shot would've gave us away!" he whispered harshly with an attitude. "You could be fucking dead right now Dylasia!"

When Trent put an emphasis on each word he gritted his teeth even harder. "Let's go."

"But I need to get Ivery…"

"Naw, what you needed was a better fucking plan." He huffed as we notice Sidney moving around a little.

"What's up fuck nigga! Ivery sent you to kill Dylasia?" Trent barked standing so close up on Sidney that he had to feel his breath.

Sydney was standing there like a deer caught in headlights after Trent snatched him up off of the ground by his shirt. His eyes were nearly bulging out of their sockets.

"Look, I told you why I came. I never wanted to hurt you Dylasia," Sidney whined as he put up his hands to guard his face. Like a bullet couldn't get through there and tear his ass up! Humph.

His little act of sympathy was beginning to work, especially after I got a glance of his face. It looked like he had some bruises.

"Don't get weak bitch!" I tried to convince myself as I studied Sydney's demanor before I aimed my pistol at him. "Whose side are you on

Sidney? The choice is yours and you don't have long to decide."

"Are you sure we will be safe this time Dylasia?" Sydney asked moving foward into the moonlight allowing me to access his damages even further.

As bad as I felt for Sydney, I had no sympathy for him any longer. He had several opportunities to take them niggas out yet he let them overpower him. A gullible person like him didn't have an ounce of loyalty in his blood. He had proven that shit one too many times...

"Damn did he do this to you?" I quizzed with my face screwed up once I noticed his right eye was closed shut. Sydney nodded and lowered his head in shame.

"Help me take him to my car Trent. You follow me in his... And Sydney this is your last chance at a new start, grow some damn balls dude please."

"Wrong, his last chance was when he drew down on you!" Trent mumbled as he grabbed onto both sides of Sydney's face and snapped his neck quickly to the left. "Just think about him being like a wounded dog. I just put him out of his misery. Now turn your head."

"For what?" I whispered and rotated my body away from him. It only lasted for a few seconds though, because after that I was peeking like a motherfucker.

"Why are you stripping him down like that?"

"You know I would tell you to go home and meet me there, but I know you wouldn't go. Yo ass would be still out here looking for Ivery. Now what if he caught you just like this faggot ass motherfucker? Then what Dy?" Trent fussed as he gathered all Sydney's clothes and bundled them up then stuck them under his arm. "Now I gotta babysit you and shit because you want to run around like you Wonder Woman or some shit."

Trent snatched me up by the arm and drug me to the car. His was parked right behind the car I drove. "You followed me here?"

"You better be glad I did!" he smirked before opening up the door for me. "I need you to take off all your clothes."

"Right here?" I asked frowning up as I took my time stripping down to nothing.

"Hurry up!" Trent gritted as he went into the trunk and got a long jacket then threw it at me. "Go straight to the fucking house Dy! Can I trust you to do that?"

"But..."

"Go! We don't have time for this right now!" Trent snapped getting madder at me than I had ever seen him get.

I took heed real quick and followed his instructions without another peep; naked and all.

Chapter 27

When I got back to the house I went and checked on my grandmother. I made it to her room to open the door and found it empty. I stared down on the bed at her bible and smiled. "I wish you were him Big Mama but I know you're having a good time on your date!"

Oh how I needed was a hug from her and I knew that I would feel a little better. All I could think about was me getting killed that night and leaving my grandmother all alone. No, I wasn't thinking at all when I went to meet Ivery alone. Bad thing was, I didn't even know if he showed up or not. I didn't know where he was.

I sighed deeply as I closed her door back and went upstairs to shower and change. When I got out, Trent was standing in the bedroom with his arms folded.

"You are so lucky right now!" Trent smirked and shook his head.

"Why?"

"Because right now all I want to do is choke yo ass out but I would never put my hands on you and disrespect you like that." Trent responded as he brushed by me harshly and went to clean up.

"Damn, I really fucked up this time!" I thought silently as I climbed into the bed. "But shit, we still didn't get Ivery!"

I dared bring that shit up to Trent, especially when he came back out of the bathroom with that same scowl on his face. I was scared to say shit.

Trent didn't even look at me. He just shut off the lights and climbed in the bed with me. He even turned his back. I felt so bad that I didn't know how to react.

"I'm sorry," I whispered.

At first Trent didn't respond. I waited for a few seconds then wrapped my arms around him from behind. "I'm sorry baby. I really am."

After taking two deep breaths, he turned to me and held me tightly. "We just went through this Dy. You can't keep scaring me like this. You keep flying off by yourself, trying to handle shit by yourself is gonna get you killed. Don't you give a fuck about me and your grandmother? Huh Dy? Do you?"

"I do baby but I wasn't thinking..."

"Fuck that Dy! Just promise me that you won't do it again."

"I won't..."

"Yeah, you said that shit last time and look at yo ass!" Trent sighed in defeat but continued to hold me.

The frustration hug began to turn into an embrace of love as Trent ran his hands down my back until they reached my behind. That started some shit right there.

I knew I was in for a pounding instead of making passionate love and I was alright with that. I was sure we both needed to release some things. At least I knew that I did...

It was short but fulfilling so I had no complaints and by the way Trent was snoring afterwards, I knew he had none either...

****

We woke up the next morning smelling food cooking. "I thought she wouldn't be back until at least noon?"

I looked at the clock and noticed that it was after one in the afternoon. Trent was still sleep.

"Baby, you know what time it is?"

"Naw, what time is it?" he repeated as he rolled out of the bed and rushed to the bathroom holding his dick like he had to piss.

While he was in there, his business cell began to ring. I started to answer it but Trent was already on his way to it.

"Agent Santiago," he answered.

There was a brief moment of silence before he spoke again. "So he's in Florida?"

After another pause Trent went on. "So you're going to bring him in the day of the court proceedings?"

Trent paced back and forth as he listened carefully on the phone.

"Okay, and if you guys let him slip away this time could you please give me a heads up immediately. I can't keep putting my family in danger!"

It truly touched my heart to hear Trent to refer to me and my grandmother as family. I guess he really did love me.

Disconnecting his call, Trent set his phone down and came and hugged me. "I guess you heard all that huh?"

"Yeah I did." I replied with a half-smile.

"Yeah, maybe we can live in peace hopefully until next month when the trial starts." Trent sighed.

"They already set a date?"

"I know right?" he continued as he gestured me to come with him. "Let's not worry about that right now. Let's go see what Big Mama is cooking up."

We both went to the kitchen to some music playing and it wasn't even gospel. It was some slow song by Aretha Franklin. I didn't recognize it, but I knew her voice anywhere.

"Look at ya grandmother!" Trent whispered as we watched Big Mama twist her hips and throw her hands in the air as she sang along with Aretha.

"She can sang too!" Trent laughed. "She's seriously blowing!"

I giggled as I nudged him in the side. "Quit talking about my grandmother. She's been singing in the choir since she was three years old!"

"You lyin'!" Trent said sounding amazed.

"No, she's not! I was quite the singer back in the day!" Big Mama bragged as she continued to belt out each and every note with precision. All the while she was still frying some pork chops to go with the potatoes and eggs she had cooking at the same time.

"So what's going on with the case?" my grandmother asked.

Trent went ahead and filled her in as he took out some plates and utensils.

"So that means I can go home and sleep in my own bed? Oh, not that the one here isn't more comfortable, but there's nothing like being in your own home."

"Sure Big Mama."

"Yeah, and you can take the car too. I know you were having problems with yours." Trent offered.

"Yes, poor thing needs to be put to rest. One day the Lord will bless me with a new one."

"Well consider yourself blessed." Trent laughed as he grabbed the keys off of the counter and handed them to her.

"What you mean by that?" she asked not quite understanding.

"It means that you can keep the car."

"Are you talking about that bright shiny new thing that has that plush interior and all those fancy gadgets?" she asked with tears in her eyes as she clutched the keys tightly.

"Yes, that one Big Mama," Trent smiled as he reached out to hug her.

She squeezed him as tight as she could and rocked his body from side to side, even though he was nearly twice her size. "Thank you so much grandson."

Yeah, I caught how she threw that 'grandson' in there. She thought she was slick…

Chapter 28

Two hours later my grandmother was gone. I really didn't want her to leave because I loved having her around.

"So, what you want to do tonight?" Trent asked as he gave me the eye.

Even though I enjoyed making love to him, that wasn't what I was in the mood for. I wanted to go out to eat and a movie; something really simple. I could get some of that afterwards.

Well, we wound up going to Pappadeaux's to get some bomb ass fried alligator and oysters. The food was delicious.

"Did you decide on the movies and check the times?"

"Yes, I want to see the new Barbershop and it's playing at the Harkin's Theater at Park West over on Northern and the 101." I told him as I doubled checked on my cell. "We have thirty minutes to get there."

When we arrived it was a long line and I was complaining as soon as we pulled up. I was highly upset because it was still hot outside. Good thing was, when it was over I could truly say it was worth the wait.

"Where to next?" Trent asked full of energy.

"Home! I'm tired," I said yawing as we walked to the car. "Matter of fact I'm about to take a nap in on the way.

I did just that and before I knew it, we were back at the house. "Damn, was I snoring?"

"Hell yeah, but you looked so beautiful the way that you were drooling that I didn't want to wake you," he teased as he got out the car.

I wiped the side of my mouth with the back of my hand and shook my head as I pulled down the visor and looked into the mirror. I was a hot ass mess for real.

"Come on," Trent said as he stood outside my side of the car and opened the door. "You alright?"

"Yeah, I'm awake now," I yawned again while trailing behind Trent.

As I walked up the few stairs, I saw something laying on the porch. Trent got to it before me and picked it up. I quickly snatched the scarf out of his hands and saw something that looked like blood on it.

"This is Big Mama's scarf! I got this for her at the swap meet!" I cried as I held it tight and smelled it. "I can even smell her perfume."

Trent pulled his gun out and opened the door to go in. He wasn't about to leave me out there so I was right on his heels.

After checking every inch of the house, we saw that Big Mama wasn't there. We couldn't even find any evidence that she had even been back there.

"Call her right now!" Trent demanded.

While I did that, he went to car to get his business cell.

"Come on Big Mama pick up!" I shouted continuously trying to reach her. I dialed her number for the next five minutes. That was when Trent finally came back in.

"Damn, I fucked up," Trent sighed making me stop what I was doing.

"What baby? What happened?"

"I left my cell in the car while we were in the movies. It was dead."

"So?"

"So, I plugged it up to get enough of a charge to call Agent Dale."

Trent explained to me how they lost track of Ivery only to find him again in Tucson. That was only a couple of hours away.

"Damn can we live one moment in fucking peace?" he fussed as we went right back out the door.

"You didn't get ahold of Big Mama?" Trent asked as we pulled off.

"No, is that where we're going?"

"You damn straight!"

Trent was driving like a bat out of hell and breaking every traffic law known to man. I didn't say shit. I just buckled up, held on and prayed the whole ride.

I swear we made it there in record timing. I was glad because I was worried about my grandmother because she still wasn't answering the phone.

"Okay, the lights are off. Which way do you want to go in?"

"Hell, I gotta key I'm going right up in there!" I said ready to fly up in there busting caps.

I got my gun out and cocked it back. "Slow ya ass down Dy! What did I tell you?"

I paused, gave him the key and let him take the lead. "Now you can have my back."

I smirked at Trent's smart ass mouth and followed him into my grandmother's house. Right away I heard her screaming out for help.

"Lawd, lawd!" Big Mama hollered out.

Without even thinking, both Trent and I busted into my grandmother's room with our guns drawn. Big Mama hopped up off of Minister Percy so damn fast that all I saw was tits and ass when she got up. She left her friend right there with a big hard on. I couldn't fucking believe my eyes. Right when I thought I had seen it all!

Trent bolted out the room and abandoned me, leaving me standing there looking like a damn fool. My mouth was hanging wide open.

"Do you mind?" Big Mama began to clown. "I can't even get me none without some drama! I'm up in here minding my own business trying to make some drama of my own. Aint that right Percy?"

Minister Percy smiled shyly and pulled my grandmother back near him. "Get on out of here! I don't even want to know why y'all came flying up in here! Hey, why don't you both do the same thing, but in reverse?"

"Huh?" I asked confused as I held up the bloody scarf. "Where did this come from?"

"Child I must have dropped it!" she answered.

"Why does it have blood on it?"

"That's ketchup girl!" my grandmother fussed angrily. "Now if there's nothing else keep it moving. Bye Dylasia!"

I shook my head and went out the room and shut the door behind me. I really think that I was more embarrassed than my grandmother was. That right there was some crazy shit.

"Now where did he go?" I mumbled when I noticed that Trent wasn't in the house. I found him outside in the car with the engine running.

When I got in, he didn't even look at me. He just pulled off.

"What's wrong?"

"I'm traumatized, what the hell you think?"

I cracked up and thought about it. Yeah, I was too...

Chapter 29

I couldn't believe that I ran up in my grandmother's house with a dirty scarf. Hell, I thought Ivery had something to do with it since no one knew where he was.

Now here it was, over a month later and we still didn't have any answers or leads on his whereabouts. I really wanted them to find him before Malcolm had his day in court. Unfortunately it didn't quite happen that way.

"I wish Ivery's ass was here to get locked up right along with Malcolm since we weren't lucky enough to kill his ass when we had the chance!" I mumbled as we sat in the back of the courtroom.

Trent elbowed me lightly and gave me that look. He was getting pretty bold with that shit.

"All rise your honorable judge Kamille Braxton is presiding." The court Marshall announced bringing everyone to their feet as the judge took her place at the bench across from twelve jurors.

"Please be seated."

The judge then proceeded to explain how the case was going to be heard. To me it was just a bunch of blah, blah, blah.

"In the matter of the state vs. Malcolm Holmes, please come forward."

Everyone walked up to the bench.

"Please raise your right hand." The judge instructed. "Do you solemnly swear to tell the truth and nothing but the truth?"

"I do."

The judge went on to explain some more before asking, "Malcolm Holmes, how do you plead?"

"Not guilty," he said looking all pitiful. They needed to throw his ass up under the jail.

I glanced at Malcolm and turned my nose up at him. When I looked at Trent, he was doing the same.

****

Well into the court hearing, they brought out the sex tapes. I became sick to my stomach when the one with me was played. It instantly felt as if everyone in the courtroom knew it was me. I felt so humiliated and dirty. I didn't let that get to me though.

The state only had Trent and I as witnesses. Everyone else that was involved was either dead or on the run. I guess we were the fortunate ones.

Right after the video, I was asked to take the stand. I did that shit with confidence and was proud of myself when I stepped down, but not as proud as I was of Trent. He was way more intelligent than I ever imagined. The way he articulated his words was amazing.

As Trent finished, he joined me, held my hand and we walked out of the courtroom together. That was enough for one day. Unfortunately it went on for two more...

By the third day and final day of the trial, I was exhausted. I was glad that it only lasted a half day. The jury went out to deliberate while we went to lunch.

When we came back they already had a decision. That grimey motherfucker was guilty as charged!

"Let's go celebrate!" Trent said with a smile.

"Naw, I don't wanna do that until Ivery is either dead or with Malcolm!" I gritted as we went home to change. We were due to go to Big Mama's house to eat in a few hours.

When we got home, we both showered and changed clothes. With an hour or so to spare we went downstairs to chill. I was hoping to watch a few episodes of Blue Bloods, until it was time to go.

"Let me see what they're saying about Malcolm's punk ass," Trent said as we stepped into the den and he turned the TV on to the news channel.

"I think that's your cell ringing," I said looking over at his jacket.

Trent had cheese on his hands from the chips he was eating so he asked me to answer it and place it on speaker.

"Hey Agent Santiago, I got some news for you."

"Excuse my language, but please share that shit Agent Dale!"

Trent set the bag of Doritos down and got closer to the phone so he could hear.

"Well, we found Ivery..."

"Did you arrest him?"

"No..."

"What? Why not? What the hell happened?" Trent said heated.

"When we found him he was dead on arrival. Someone tortured and sliced him pretty good. It was a scene out of a horror movie."

"What?" Trent asked. My ears were standing straight up. I wanted to hear all the facts.

The agent went on and told the location and time of death. The details were unbelievable, especially what he told us about the way they found him.

"Yes, they carved the words, 'No Loyalty, No Love' into his chest." Agent Dale revealed.

Right away Trent looked at me and squinted. "Okay thanks Agent Dale. I appreciate you calling."

Trent hung up the phone on the agent and began interrogating the hell out of me. I tried my best to suppress the laughter, but I couldn't. I didn't do it though.

The look on Trent's face once he got the news was priceless. Working beside him for the last year taught me how to plan, move in silence, and execute. One thing Ivery didn't foresee was me ending is career in Miami Beach.

I found him up to his same old tricks and delivered his poison to him.

"Dy' this shit is not funny! I wanted that motherfucker dead too, but what if this all comes back to haunt us later on?... Let me guess you didn't think that far ahead, from here on out start using your brain and not your heart!" Trent was pissed with me yet again except this time I really didn't do it…

Chapter 30

Trent was going on and on about how he knew it was me that did that to Ivery, but I wasn't trying to hear nothing about Ivery! Finally a bitch could move on with her life damn. Whoever killed him I wanted to find him or her and thank them. They did us a big ass favor. Why wasn't Trent seeing it like that?"

"Man fuck them folks! No one cared how they violated my soul, so you know what if they do come knocking I'll take my chances in court because I didn't kill the man!"

I knew Trent was concerned about my safety and I appreciated him, but I honestly had nothing to do with it.

Trent gave me the side eye and left me standing there. I didn't want to beef with him over a nigga laying in the morgue so I followed behind him.

"Trent, I am not going to tell you I'm sorry for something that I didn't do. If you're mad then so be it. I'm standing here telling you the truth but obviously you're gonna believe what you want. But, when the truth comes out I want the biggest apology ever!" I fussed.

Trent ignored my words and sprayed his cologne on his wrist, dabbing a little onto his neck He was seriously giving me the silent treatment behind something I didn't do.

I took the silence for what it was worth and made my way to the kitchen. Pouring me a shot of tequila, I sent Big Mama a text letting her know that we were on our way.

Before I could down my shot of alcohol, Trent grabbed me by my waist and sat me on the counter. He was standing in front of me looking irresistible in his Ralph Lauren tank, khaki shorts, and loafers with a matching cap. I bit down on my lip and braced myself for whatever he was bringing. It was just the opposite of what I was expecting…

Cupping my chin in his hand like he always did, Trent brought my face up to his. I stared deeply into his eyes and my stomach started fluttering.

"My vow to you from this day forth is to love, cherish, honor, protect, provide, assist, cater, encourage, spoil, and tame my pussy. There are no motives or ploys. It's just you and I now and you can't get rid of me. I am in love with yo' crazy ass!" Trent said all in his feelings. I was surprised that he actually expressed how he felt right then.

"I'm speechless right now baby. I love you too, Trent." Was the only thing I managed to come up with?

The moment his lips touched mine, our hands ravaged over one another bodies passionately. I grinded my hips against his erect rod leaving his print visible enough for me to see as my pussy became wet at just the thought of an intense dick session. Instead I thought of something to satisfy us both. A little foreplay…

Unzipping Trent shorts I fondled him until I exposed his dick. Spreading my leg across the counter I scooted my pussy down just enough.

Stroking his manhood I rubbed the tip of his dick against the center of my opening. I climaxed immediately at his touch. The sensation I was receiving from his head massaging my clit sent me into another immediate orgasm.

I caressed his balls and then his shaft making sure it was nice and hard. I was giving him the best hand job he had in his life.

"Oh shit baby, right there!" Trent moaned near climaxing.

I stopped mid-stroke and rubbed the tip of his dick at my opening releasing my sweet juices all over us. "Fuck…" Trent moaned with my nipple partially in his mouth.

I knew he was ready to take me down and nail me to the cross but Big Mama was waiting on us…

****

Soon as we got there Big Mama was all over us like she hadn't seen us in years. To be honest she had spending all her time between church and Minister Percy.

We washed up and went straight to grubbing. When we finished we sat around chatting.

"Have you thought about investing into real estate young man?" Percy asked Trent as they discussed current events, politics, sports, and the stock market, some shit I knew nothing about.

I excused myself and went into the kitchen to help Big Mama clean up. That's the least I could do after she threw down on dinner. She prepared us wild rice, blackened salmon, mixed vegetables, fresh corn muffins, and for dessert we ate a lemon pound cake.

I swear that lady gave me life on the daily. "Big Mama I love you." I laid my head on her shoulder as we stood by the sink.

"I love you too. There's nothing to be afraid of Dy'…, Trent is a fine young tender who genuinely cares for and loves you. Just take it easy and what is meant to be will be." She rubbed my hair and for the first time in a long time I felt at peace.

Suddenly my grandmother got silent and walked to the drawer by the backdoor and opened it up. I watched her as she pulled out a towel with something wrapped in it.

"Can you have Trent get rid of this for me?" She asked as she walked over to me and showed me what was inside.

"Is that what I think it is?" I gasped as I closed the bloody knife and gun back up in the towel. "Big Mama, where did this stuff come from?"

"Didn't we have to stop him?" she winked as she held on to the evidence.

"Yes, but how, but when?" I whispered. "You couldn't have done it all by yourself!"

"No, she didn't and she won't have to another thing in her life alone from now on if I can help it!" Minister Percy said upon entering the kitchen and placing his arm around Big Mama.

"Hey, what's going on in here?" Trent asked as he joined us.

I took the towel from Big Mama and handed it to Trent. Then they all went into the living room to discuss what happened. I didn't go with them. Instead, I stayed in the kitchen and finished cleaning. The last thing I wanted to hear about was Ivery. He was dead and that was good enough for me.

After I put away the dishes, I took a bottle of champagne and some glasses in the front. It wasn't until that very moment did my heart skipped several beats.

Trent was holding a medium sized white box, pink roses, along with Percy holding a small pink envelope in his hand. I smiled nervously turning to look at Big Mama. She was cheesing harder than a little kid in a candy store.

"What is going on and why are y'all smiling so hard?" I grilled them.

Trent cleared his throat. "Like I told you earlier..." He handed me the roses and bent down on one knee. "Everything and more I want to be with you. I loved you from the second I laid eyes on you and I couldn't imagine living a day without you by my side like Bonnie & Clyde. Dylasia, will you be mine forever and marry me?"

Trent tried his best not to choke up. Hell I was already crying like a little bitch.

"Here baby," Trent said as he removed the top of the box. The shine coming from my ring damn near blinded me because it was so iced up.

"Yes I will marry you Trenton Santiago!"

I was beyond ecstatic and never in a million years did I think that a little ghetto hood chick with class from Cali would marry a nigga of Trent's caliber.

"How do you know my ring size?" I quizzed Trent as he slid the two carat chocolate diamond engagement ring onto my finger.

"It's my job to know everything about you." Trent replied kissing me softly on the lips.

"This is for you and Dylasia on a new start of your beautiful journey." Percy handed me the card. I opened it up and it was a deed of a eight bedroom house in Scottsdale and a check for $25,000." I turned to my grandmother who had tears running down her face.

"I want you to be happy, Dylasia and live your life to the fullest. We're leaving tonight for a cruise to the Bahamas. I love you and go after your dreams no matter how hard it may get never settle."

Chapter 31

Trent was a nervous wreck the morning of the ceremony and he was making my ass hurt. He was running around the house undecided on what to wear when I swear we just went over that shit a week before.

The mayor and city of Phoenix were honoring Trent. It was for his bravery, heroism, and success in taking down some major hitters in the human traffic arena in the metropolitan district of Phoenix.

I was proud of him as I fixed his tie and admired his four o'clock shadow peaking on his chin. Not only was he receiving a key to the city, we were set to open up for business the following week.

"Come on baby, we gotta go!" I yelled upstairs only to find out that Trent was already in the car waiting on me.

Soon as I got my second leg in he was already taking off. He did a twenty minute drive in ten. Yeah, he was driving was too fast.

"Well, here we are," I smiled up at Trent who kissed me before he took his assigned position.

When he turned around, I glanced over at him and felt like the luckiest girl in the world. Despite what I had to go through many blessings came from it.

"Awwww look at my man!"

Trent stood proudly with his head held high next to the Sergeant, Chief of Police, and the Mayor.

I sat out in the audience with Big Mama, Percy, and Trent's parents, who I finally met, as the

Mayor announced Trent's name. When he stepped to him, he held out the key to the city and placed it in my fiancée's hand.

Everyone cheered and was ready to celebrate, but not me and Trent. We were ready to start moving into our new house.

I ran my mouth all the way there I was so excited. It was my first time owning a house and it was the proudest day of my life. Well almost....

I had three more weeks for that day to come. That was the day I would officially be 'Mrs. Santiago'.

"It is so damn big!" Trent shouted as we pulled up in the wrap-around driveway.

We both got out and stood there staring at our new house from the outside.

"What are we gonna do with all this damn space?" Trent laughed as he held my hand and led me up the stairs.

"Well, I know what one room is gonna be!" I teased ready to reveal my secret.

"What's that, an office?" Trent asked as he opened up the front door and saw the baby furniture I had delivered.

"No, a nursery!"

"What?"

"Yes baby, in six more months we are going to be parents!"

Trent lifted me up off of my feet, kissed me and then started balling like a baby. I was right along with him.

It was a brand new start to a brand new chapter in our life.

"Now I wonder what it will bring…"

The End

Trenton

&

Dylasia

Unbreakable Bond

Sneak Peek

"Attention everyone gather around!" Big Mama shouted looking fabulous in her peach one strapped dress I picked out for her.

Percy, Trent, myself, and a few friends of Trent's from the bureau, all sat around the elegant arrangement of the dinner table. As we settled down Big Mama cleared her throat.

"I want to take this time to thank Trent for a superb job with the F.B.I. You are truly one of a kind son. Also congratulations on your new business venture. To my beautiful granddaughter Dylasia, I am so proud of the woman you are blossoming into. I wish you and Trent many blessings. Just hurry up and have me a baby. I love you both to pieces." Big Mama spoke getting emotional.

"Thanks Big Mama we love you too!" Trent replied scooting his chair back he stood up to embrace both of us. "That's already done! Dy's pregnant!"

"Oh yes!" my grandmother yelled out. "Cheers!"

"Cheers!" Trent chimed raising his glass.

"Cheers!" We shouted in unison.

The celebration dinner was perfect as Trent and I mingled with our guests. The DJ was playing all the latest music and I wanted to dance. Not to mention Trent had me feeling on top of the world as I glanced down at my two carat chocolate diamond Neil Lang engagement ring.

We finally were getting to a life we deserved. It was slowly getting back to normal and I wanted to enjoy each day not worrying about tomorrow.

"Excuse us for a moment. Trent come dance with me." I grabbed his hand before he could refuse and led him to the floor.

Beyoncé's get me bodied song blared from the speakers. I was ready to tear some shit up!

I popped and swayed my hips, all on Trent. It was like I was giving him his own private show. Our guests were cheering us on as a few others got out there with us.

"You know up until I met you, I gave up on loving another woman and tucked my heart away. Despite the way we met, I wouldn't change one moment that I have had you in my life. You make a man want to evolve, be more, and have more in life. I love you Dy'." Trent spoke wrapping me into his arms as we swayed to the slow jam.

"I love you too Trenton, let's go cut this cake and get out of here. We have a flight to Washington at five in the morning." I replied glancing at my watch checking it once more before giving him a quick kiss.

"After you my gorgeous fiancée." Trent interlocked our fingers and headed for the buffet table where the cake was placed.

I tapped the microphone to make sure it was on. "Trent and I thank each and every one of you for supporting us. Hope you enjoyed yourselves like we have, but unfortunately duty calls. Blessings."

Trent sliced the cake leaving everyone to go for their own troubles. Trent phone sounded off distracting him just as I was about to kiss him. From the way his posture changed, I knew it was news he wasn't hoping to hear.

He pulled me into him and I prepared myself for the worse. I knew exactly how DMX felt! Here we go again!

"We may have our first client for Santiago Investigative Services. I'll fill you in on the specifics when we get in the car. You ready my love?" Trent asked placing his hand in the center of my back.

"I am."

Trent led us to the entrance of the Marillo Luxe Hotel where our chauffeur awaited. After the Mayor of Phoenix gave Trent a key to the city we were treated like royalty.

"Where to Sir?" The driver asked as he emerged into traffic.

"District Nine Precinct off Van Buren." Trent informed while taking my hand in his.

"I just got a call from an old partner of mine. His niece was kidnapped in Tucson...By the Sonoita Cartel. The mother is waiting with Detective Olson. The girl name is Jasmine Harris, age 15, Spanish and African-American, we'll get more details once we get there."

"I don't know what or how to feel. We just got our lives stable and here this shit comes. I'm not trying to lose you or myself fucking with them cheese eating, sick fuckers!" I spat becoming vexed.

"Listen baby if no one understands how you feel I do. But I can't turn away from my calling in life. You are now an advocate for human trafficking and predators like the Sonoita Cartel. Don't be afraid to help other people. If you don't want to work on this case with me that is perfectly fine." Trent smirked gazing into my eyes. "You will stay in the office or hotel while I go out in the field. The only reason why I'm letting you go while you're pregnant is because I need you with me."

I understood, but still had nightmares of Ivery raping me. I didn't know if I could go back into it so soon, especially when we had no idea who was now running the Cartel...

Made in the USA
Columbia, SC
06 September 2021